Turn Back Time

and other

Time Travel Tales

ALSO BY MARY ELLEN SPRINGSTEEN

The Universal Donor

In The Name Of Beauty

Cyber Match

Turn Back Time

and other

Time Travel Tales

MARY ELLEN SPRINGSTEEN

ISBN-13:
978-0999246306 (Mary Ellen Springsteen)

ISBN-10:
0999246305

Cover Design by Eric Labacz, LabaczDesign.com

Cover Photos by Ray Hennessy and Alex Blajan on Unsplash.com

Author Photo by Bill Gardner Jr., www.alpinedreamsphotography.com

DEDICATION

To my centurion aunt and true sage, Tillie Carey. Rest in peace, Aunt Tillie, and until we meet again, may God hold you in the palm of His hand.

Table of Contents

Home

Navi, my pet name for the GPS system in my car, and I were at odds again. I lost my temper with her when she directed me into the extreme left lane of a major intersection and then told me to turn right. Her response to my verbal abuse was the silent treatment.

So, I end up stranded in the middle of nowhere, totally lost, out of gas, food and water, with a dead cell phone and laptop. Meanwhile, my new business client thinks I'm a no-show.

From the moment that I accidentally entered this unmarked road, I did not see a single sign indicating the name of the road, the town, or even a speed limit. No lights, no intersections, or evidence of any type of life.

Hoping to be spotted eventually, I popped the car hood, tied a chamois car cloth to the side view mirror facing the road, and patiently waited for someone, anyone to pass by. Hopefully some Good Samaritan will help me find fuel or at the very least call for help.

One hour, two hours passed; there wasn't a soul in sight. My eyelids grew heavy, my throat parched as I sat waiting in the driver's seat. Suddenly, I heard what sounded like a small truck slowing down and stopping directly behind me.

A mid-seventyish man wearing a straw hat stepped out of the truck and walked over to my car. "Say, fellah, you need help?" he asked.

"Sure do. I'm out of gas, lost and late for a critical business meeting. May I please make some calls with your cell phone? I need fuel and should call my business client."

"Sorry, Mister, I don't have a cell phone. But I have enough gas in my pickup to get you going. You can follow me to the filling station."

"Man, I owe you big time! My name is Mark Jensen. I sell solar systems to businesses on the East Coast."

"Howdy, Mark. I'm Jonas Turner, and I own the best horse ranch around."

"Around where, may I ask? I have no idea where we are."

"This road you're on is a temporary service road built for the big tractor trailer rigs. It takes the big rigs past the steep hills and then reconnects further down with the main road. We're actually in the outskirts of my town, 'Home.' "

"Your hometown, which is?"

"Home. Home *is* the name of my hometown. The founding settlers couldn't think of a better name, I reckon. They always called it Home and so it stuck. Last tally, our population was fifty and a couple of newborns are on the way." Jonas beamed proudly.

Fifty? Why, more than fifty people live on my street alone.

"This was supposed to be a ninety-minute road trip, about seventy-five miles between my house in Princeton, New Jersey and a business in Allentown, Pennsylvania. A straight run. Somehow, I messed up. I haven't seen a single sign of life until you pulled up."

Jonas emptied the contents of his gas can into my tank. I followed him to fill up and hopefully call my client. It seemed like an eternity before we reached the gas station. I bought fuel but couldn't make any calls as the station didn't have a phone. Nor did the station owner or any other customers have cell phones. Odd.

My new friend would not take a cent for helping me. I gratefully accepted his offer to get me back on course to my destination. We were leaning over my car hood, going over a map, when the sky appeared purplish-black while the road map was threatening to become a flyaway kite.

"Storm's coming in. Could be a twister. Sky's nearly black. Trust me, Mark, you're better off not driving in this. Folks have gone missing out in these remote parts. Listen, I should tend to my horses and you need a place to wait out the storm. So, how's about we head out to my ranch now? You can eat and rest until the storm lets up. It might be a few hours, maybe longer. You can take the spare room; stay as long as you like."

"That's mighty generous of you, Jonas. You're right. I'm better off waiting a bit. Thanks."

Is he for real? A total stranger… Who makes this kind of offer to a stranger?

Between the sky and the wind gusts, I had no other choice than to follow Jonas to his ranch. His spread was situated on ten plus acres. It included a log cabin home, a barn that housed ten horses, a fenced in corral, and a storage shed. I helped him tend to his horses and prepare for the storm.

Jonas lost his wife to cancer a few years back and managed to run the ranch without any outside help. He prepared a pot of delicious soup on his rustic wood burning stove. We joked and swapped stories over dinner. Jonas beat me at a game of checkers and I took him at a hand of cards.

Wind gusts howled louder by the minute. The power went out, leaving us with lanterns for light and the stove for heat. We lost reception on the battery radio. I wanted to check my messages and talk to my girlfriend, Susan, but, how could I?

The hour grew late and the storm showed no signs of retreating. I took Jonas up on his previous offer and bunked in the spare room for the night. The ranch offered all the amenities of home such as heat, running cold and hot water, a fully equipped bathroom, lights, and a wood burning stove.

I couldn't help but notice, however, the absence of any type of phone, TV, CD or DVD player, camera, video game, computer, or Internet. Odd, no?

I awoke to brilliant sunshine pouring in through the guest room window and the aroma of fresh coffee brewing and crackling bacon and eggs sizzling on Jonas's wood stove.

"Man, does breakfast ever smell good and the storm has finally passed!" I said.

"Yup, sky's all clear. I lucked out—just three busted fence posts. 'Course my horses were shook up, but they calmed down. Power should be back by tomorrow. After breakfast, I can show you around town a bit. Spend the day if you like—don't know your schedule."

"I feel awful about missing my appointment and not making important contacts, but things were out of my control. Once I get back, I'll deal with things. Meanwhile, I'm game for a tour. I just won't stay late. I'll pack up my car in case I need to take off before you head home."

Jonas and I walked the short distance to the center of town. He pointed out several family run shops: an old-fashioned barber shop with a traditional pole out front; a bakery; and a confectionary ice cream parlor equipped with vintage counter stools, chilled metal ice cream cups, and a working juke box.

The general store had a creaky, crooked wooden floor, a huge pickle barrel, and assorted household items. A small room in the back of this store was a fully functioning Western Union office. The post office was quaint, circa 1950s. The town's only school covered kindergarten through twelfth grade (K-12).

A very old church with a pristine white steeple and bell tower adorned the corner. Sunday service was about to begin. The townspeople were arriving on foot. A rosy cheeked, young boy was in his glory as he cheerfully fulfilled his ritual of ringing the church bell.

For a moment, I stared at the carefree boy in awe as if I was watching an old movie or reading an old classic. But I was doing neither. No, this was real. I was here, in the present. I wanted to see more.

"Mark, since we're here, would you like to see our church? You need not stay for the service. The building dates back over a hundred years."

"Yeah, let's go in."

Jonas and I walked into the church and sat in a pew near the back. The sun shining through stained glass windows on both sides created a shimmering rainbow effect throughout. The wooden pews were polished to perfection.

Pipe organ music played a beautiful chorus. The congregation filtered in and the service began. When the time came to offer each other the sign of peace, I was treated kindly. A stranger to all but Jonas, people shook my hand and smiled genuinely.

As service let out, Jonas mentioned that he had committed to a community luncheon and asked if I'd like to attend. He said that at least once a month, they gather after church service for a pot luck lunch. It gives them a chance to catch up, see how everyone's doing and help each other out.

"Thanks for the invite, Jonas. Sure, I'll go for a little while. I really do need to head out soon, though."

"Of course, you do. I'm glad you decided to join us. Besides, you need to eat lunch some place, right?"

"Right."

A hearty breakfast followed by a picnic lunch. Folks work and play hard. No fad diets here.

Everyone met at the local park, the perfect setting for a fun-filled afternoon. The pot luck spread was unbelievable. All the food was either home grown or homemade and included finger-licking, fried chicken, plump sausages, salads, fruits, vegetables, deviled eggs, buttered corn on the cob, breads, cookies, cakes and pies, ice cream, apple cider, and freshly brewed coffee.

"Jonas, how did the townspeople prepare all this food with the power outage?" I asked.

"Doc has a generator and a few homes still have power. Folks take turns making their dishes. We're a good team."

"You sure are."

A horse shoe competition was going strong. Another group played cards. Kids played tag, catch, hide and seek, and hop scotch—batteries not required. Young men and women were strumming their guitars and singing while accompanied by keyboard and harmonica players. I saw one of the adults filling balloons with water for a balloon toss, no doubt. A potato sack race was assembling.

Fifth Avenue's influence had not reached Home. Everyone wore well made, classic style clothes; their clothing wasn't trendy or dated. Even the hairstyles looked current. But then, anything goes with hair nowadays. They didn't follow a dress code or all dress exactly alike by any means. I applaud whoever made their clothing. Perhaps their town tailor and seamstress made most of their clothes to order. No doubt, some residents also sewed.

Amidst all the comradery, I observed once more the absence of any electronics or Wi-Fi. Everyone made me feel at home. I joined in some of the games and got to know the adults and the kids.

This town was quite unique, the likes of which I have never seen. The locals were a tightly knit unit, but they were not associated with a commune or cult. The sole church was non-denominational. Everyone simply gathered to pray.

The townspeople practiced the barter system. Only a couple of miles long, a minimal number of businesses serviced the residents. For example, they had only one medical doctor (a general practitioner), barber shop, shoe cobbler, bakery, post office, beauty parlor, seamstress, tailor, general store, and so forth.

There were no rules in place against competition. The people formed a consensus that they only needed one of each type of establishment. Should this arrangement no longer work, the town would deal with it.

The business owners trained apprentices to assist with the daily business tasks and take the reins when they needed time off. When a business owner wished to retire, he or she would either pass the business on to willing family members or apprentices or sell it to a prospective buyer.

I was amazed to discover some things that Home did not have: a government, for one; a mayor or city council; property or state taxes; unions; a court or jail system; police; or a hospital.

"Please explain," I asked a young man named Sean, "without any government or law enforcement, how do you create rules for living? Who protects you from crime? How do you collect benefits during tough times? What if someone needs a hospital?"

"Well, for starters," Sean said, "we don't need rules here. We have mutual respect so we don't commit crimes against others. We look out for each other and help anyone in need.

"If my house burned down, the whole community would unite and provide my family and me with temporary shelter and food while the townspeople build my family's new home. The same helping hand would be extended for illness or death in the family.

"So, you see, we don't collect benefits here; we take care of each other. We've been blessed overall with good health. Sure, people get sick, people die. Doc and his assistants cover our medical needs. There's a major hospital just a few miles out of town."

"Were all of you born and raised here?" I asked. "Do you ever admit outsiders?"

"Well, some of us were born here. Others married locals and settled down here and raised their families. And some folks just showed up out of the blue and stayed. We all enjoy living here. Home's not like most towns, so I hear. It's not for everyone."

I was blown away by these revelations. Careful not to overstay my welcome and saddened that I must depart, I bid my farewells to everyone.

"Now, don't be a stranger to us, Mark. You're welcome in Home anytime. No need to *phone* ahead." Jonas chuckled, his eyes twinkling at his unintended pun.

"Thanks for everything, Jonas. You've been a true friend, something quite rare these days. And thank you *all* for being such gracious hosts to a lost stranger. Getting lost this time was one of the best things I've ever done."

I'll start charging my phone on my return trip. Once I'm back, I'll explain my situation to everyone. The way I see it, if this client refuses my company's business, they don't deserve our business. But you know the old saying, "The customer is always right." I'll just hope for the best; I must meet my quota.

Yesterday, my world was crumbling. In retrospect, perhaps I was meant to get lost so I would meet Jonas and experience Home. I believe that things happen for a reason. No sense dwelling on this.

Prior to leaving, I plugged in my car phone charger. Navi and I reconciled. I liked the song playing on the radio, so I asked my car to upload it to my cell phone.

I drove along peacefully the first couple of miles, smiling broadly as I mentally relived the past two days. Suddenly an old familiar song came into my head and I started singing it at the top of my lungs, changing the words as I drove along.

"Country road, take me *Home*, to the place I want to be. Pennsylvania, Pennsylvania, take me *home*, country road."

Sadly, my peaceful journey was destined to be interrupted. Once my phone had a few bars, the calls wouldn't cease. I came close to heaving it out the window. Text messages were appearing on my dashboard display also. My supervisor demanded a detailed explanation of where I've been, why the no-show on Saturday, yada, yada, yada.

The tension was rising as I played back Susan's messages. Throughout all her rantings, she never once expressed concern for my welfare. Her final message shrieked coldly through my car speakers, "Mark, this is the *last* time I'm calling. We need to *talk*," followed by a dial tone.

How comforting, Susan. Do you miss me or care about me at all? I could be seriously injured or dead, for all you know.

I accidentally set off my car alarm at a rest stop. That was fun. My mind kept escaping back to my awesome weekend. Suddenly, my brain clicked. I took the very next turnaround pointing me back to Home. Navi recognized the shift in direction and proceeded to lecture me with *attitude*.

"You have altered course and are traveling in the wrong direction. Turn around at the next jug handle, five hundred feet ahead to correct your course. I repeat, turn around at the next..."

I was at my wit's end with Navi. Recalling my previous explosion, I gritted my teeth and counted to ten. Then I started to feel like a slacker, shirking my responsibilities, running from my supervisor and my girlfriend. Navi was right as usual. I should turn around now, man up, make amends, and do the right thing...

As I unlocked my house door, I suddenly realized that I had misplaced my only house alarm remote, probably buried deep within my luggage. To top this off, I couldn't recall my code. Blaring ear drum dissolving sirens broke the silence. I raced to answer my ringing house phone, knowing full well that the caller was my alarm monitoring company.

I explained my situation and finally convinced the alarm company that *I* was *me*. At last, they silenced the alarm and gave me a new temporary code. Several irate neighbors stopped by to *thank* me for disrupting their sleep or favorite TV shows. Somebody wanting to *help* had reported my *break-in* to the police because two patrol cars screeched up out front. This had all the earmarks of a very long night.

*** * ***

Skimming through the TV channels, I found over a thousand channels with nothing on. My house phone had twenty plus messages: six from Susan, three from my mom, and one from one of my credit card banks. The rest looked like telemarketers.

I decided to forego listening to Susan's messages until she and I spoke. My mom's messages were mostly filled with sobbing because I missed my regular Sunday phone call. Way past her bedtime, I recorded a message to myself to call her the next day.

The bank had been desperately trying to reach me since Saturday about a possible identity threat to my credit card account. Thankfully I didn't need to use this credit card as they placed a fraud alert on the account unbeknownst to me.

At this point, having my identity stolen may be a godsend. Between my business and personal email accounts, I have seven hundred *urgent* messages. And then there are my online banking, PayPal, Facebook, Instagram, and Twitter accounts to check out.

So good to be back …

Reflecting on my recent adventure, I daydream about the town with the absence of any type of governing body, law enforcement, property or state taxes, phones, electronics, or Internet. Bizarre as this sounds, I prefer to view this as home. Oh, my dear, sweet Navi, I beg of you, please take me *Home* ...

Politics as Usual Circa 2525

United States of America, 2525

Dana Nelsen had an extremely good feeling about today. She recently threw her name into the ring of presidential candidates. This wouldn't have been possible centuries ago. It had nothing to do with her gender. Ten female presidents previously served. Race, religion, heritage, or sexual orientation was also irrelevant. They had all been represented over the years.

Political parties started shutting down as more and more citizens transferred their affiliations to independent candidates. Most independent candidates were not wealthy and abhorred political favors. They ran frugal campaigns utilizing all free and affordable promotional avenues. Social media, interactive website blogs, creating and distributing their own flyers, and public appearances–they did it all on shoestring budgets.

Every state offered their resident candidates free TV and radio time slots with national or international coverage. The candidates could focus on their platforms without travel expenses and other stressors. Dana Nelsen had no money, limited credit and was new to the political world. These were no longer obstacles.

Dana was the middle child of divorcee, Kate Nelsen. They lived in a low-income housing complex in Trenton, New Jersey. Kate worked two jobs most of the year. She passed her hardworking genes on to her children. They applied themselves in school and worked part-time when school was in session and full-time during their school breaks.

Kate's oldest, Brad, was a licensed plumber who recently opened his own business. Shellie, her youngest, earned a teaching degree and taught in their local elementary school system.

Dana frugally saved for college and received several academic scholarships. This lightened her burden. Still, as a full-time college student and part-time paralegal, she lived frugally.

Five years ago, she earned her law degree from New York University School of Law and passed the bar exam with flying colors. She was approached by several prestigious out of state law firms but elected to join Larsen & Reed in Princeton, New Jersey. Perhaps the Big Apple or the Pacific coastline would entice her at some point down the road—just not today.

Dana was still living with her mother, catching up on her bills, helping with household expenses, and growing her savings. It was time to spread her wings, live on her own. She also wanted to help her mother retire.

Forget about the myth that law students were all about the money. Dana would need to pay off any outstanding school loans and other debts of course, but she was anxious to take on some pro bono work. She never forgot her roots and had a soft spot for the underdog.

*** * ***

Dana has a time slot on New Jersey Focus TV this evening. The station is airing this broadcast worldwide. This is her chance to present her platform and show the public what she's all about. The host's questions are never rehearsed. She must remain cool and steady on her feet throughout the show.

*** * ***

She left work early and made a quick stop at Express Copy to pick up her campaign flyers before heading home.

A male clerk greeted Dana at the counter, "Hi, Dana. Your flyers look great." He placed a flyer on the counter for her approval.

"Wow, they're perfect. Good job, you guys."

"Thanks. We're all anxious to see you on TV tonight—excited?"

"I'll say. My first time live with *no* rehearsals or scripting."

"No lines to forget then. Break a leg. On second thought, just be yourself. You can do it."

"Thanks, see you soon."

*** * ***

The house was empty when Dana arrived home.

Mom must still be working. I know she'll catch the show. She's more psyched than I am...

Her best interview suit hung waiting on her bedroom door and her conservative pumps could pass a general's inspection. She showered and carefully dressed for her interview.

*** * ***

New Jersey Focus TV, Trenton, New Jersey

Dana entered the lobby of the TV station and was buzzed into the restricted area filled with monitors, computers, lights, cell phones ringing, and people racing back and forth ...

"Ms. Nelsen, welcome," show host, Paul Young said.

"Hello, Mr. Young. I'm honored to meet you."

"The pleasure is all mine. Please, call me Paul," he said as they shook hands.

"Sure thing, Paul. Please call me Dana."

"You've promoted your candidacy so well, Dana. Everyone's familiar with your background and campaign. You could very well be the next president of the United States."

Dana's warm smile minimized her blushing.

Get used to it. You're running for president and yes, you could win.

Within five minutes, Dana was seated with a cape over her clothes. The crew rushed in and perfected her hair and makeup.

"Five ... Four ...Three ... Two ... One ...And we're on the air."

"Good evening," Paul said. "Welcome to New Jersey Focus TV. I'm your host, Paul Young, and I have a very special guest tonight. Her name is Dana Nelsen. She's an attorney with Larsen & Reed, Princeton, New Jersey and is running for the office of president of the United States of America. Ladies and gentlemen, please welcome Dana Nelsen."

The audience cheered and applauded as Dana made her way to the podium. She did a quick tense-release, inhale, exhale and found her focal point in the audience.

"Thank you, Paul," Dana said, "for inviting me on your show. I'm honored to be here and to speak to all of you."

Focus. Respond clearly, completely. No bluffing. Either answer the questions or state that you'll follow-up.

The audience applauded for several minutes. Dana beamed at them. Then she saw her in the first row. Her mother was clapping and cheering and crying.

I knew she'd make it ...

"Welcome, Dana," Paul said. "Viewers, we do not script our presidential candidates. Instead, we select random questions from our database, our viewers, and current events.

"Ms. Nelsen, my first question for you is this. If you were elected president, what improvements, if any, would you make to our education system?"

"Great question. If I was elected president, education would be one of my top priorities. I've researched our current education system over the years. My findings included progressions and setbacks.

"The introduction of computers brought new pathways to knowledge. With each technological advancement came increased pathways. The *Information Superhighway* was the ultimate gateway.

"We all benefit from today's technologies, and yet, we all suffer. I don't propose eliminating technologies, but I do believe that we also must relearn some pre-electronic routines such as cursive writing, spelling, and phonics. Money management training should be added to every high school's curriculum.

"As for social skills, Facetime is especially great for connecting with people at a distance. Face to face time, however, is equally important. Remember, electronic devices keep us closer to people at a distance but also distance us from the person next to us.

"What would we do without electronic signatures? Still, shouldn't we also be literate in longhand or cursive writing? Without it, we cannot even sign our own names or read historical documents.

"Then there's reading. Over time, we've gradually lost touch with reading. Everything's in soundbites. Students, workers, retirees all need to make time to read. Thanks to our English language fluency requirement for citizenship, literacy is rising. Government and legal forms are no longer needed in multiple languages. These are a few of my educational recommendations. For a more detailed list, please visit my website."

The audience clapped enthusiastically.

"Well done, Dana," Paul said. "Now, let's move on to my next question. Unemployment rates have remained very low for the last several centuries. How do you plan to maintain this level?"

"Our national low unemployment figures clearly indicate that we're on the right track. My only recommendations would be to increase incentives to workers desiring early retirement. There's no reason why a retiree can't work part-time or pursue personal interests. I would also grant better tax breaks to employers who treat their employees well and grow within the United States as opposed to off-shoring. I don't suggest banning all imports, but I'd offer more incentives to spend locally."

Again, the audience applauded.

"It looks like we have time for one more question," Paul said. "Decades ago, the house and senate did not have term limits. They, along with the president and staff, received full benefits and security protection for life. As president, would you promote modifying our current practices?"

Dana paused momentarily before speaking. "That was the norm back in the day. Public servants also received better benefits in and out of office than the private sector. At least now, basic health insurance is equal for all. As the saying goes, 'If it isn't broken, don't fix it.' We're talking about government service jobs, not lifetime careers.

"Private industry employees aren't covered for life. Why should public service employees deserve this? Government employees work for the public; it's not, the other way around. When they leave their assignments, they return to their private lives and cover their own expenses. My platform is explained in detail on my website. Feel free to contact me with any questions or concerns."

"Well, folks," Paul said, "this concludes tonight's show. Thank you, Dana, our audience, and all our viewers out there. Goodnight."

The show was over, but the energy played on. The audience gave Dana a standing ovation and continued cheering and clapping as they vacated the room.

Dana met up with her mother backstage.

"Dana, I'm so proud of you," her mother said. They hugged tightly.

"Thanks, Mom. I felt butterflies the first couple of minutes. I was more nervous about the questions than anything else."

"Well, you came across as confident and focused. Even I didn't sense that you were nervous."

*** * ***

Dana's TV appearance was well received. Her website and social media confirmed this. New Jersey Focus TV would go around numerous times with all the New Jerseyan presidential candidates. Time permitting, they would conduct a drawing for additional shows.

Dana Nelsen and Carl Thompson were leading neck to neck. An election held today could easily result in a tie. Luckily for both candidates, there was still time.

*** * ***

New Jersey Focus TV, Trenton, New Jersey

Carl Thompson's New Jersey Focus TV time slot was about to air.

"Five ... Four ...Three ... Two ... One ...And we're on the air."

"Good evening, ladies and gentlemen, and welcome to our show. My name is Paul Young and I'm hosting tonight's show. United States of America presidential candidate, Carl Thompson is our special guest. Without further ado, please welcome Carl Thompson."

The crowd applauded as Carl stepped up to the podium and adjusted the microphone.

"Carl, it's nice to meet you," Paul said. "For starters, please tell us a little about yourself and your decision to enter this presidential race."

"First, I'd like to thank you, Paul, for having me on your show. My name is Carl Thompson. I was born in Newark, New Jersey where I completed thirteen years of public school. I accepted a college scholarship to Rutgers University and completed my Master's degree in Political Science seven years ago.

"Following graduation, I began teaching in high schools and junior colleges throughout New Jersey. In addition, I performed pro bono work for New Jersey elections and public affairs committees.

"Politics are in my blood. My great-grandfather was the mayor of Newark in 2300. Several of my aunts, uncles and, cousins have served terms in the house and senate.

"Besides working full-time, I devote as much time as possible to volunteering throughout my community and numerous charitable organizations.

"If I was elected president, I would corroborate with my team of experts. We'd perform in-depth evaluations of our current government practices, determine if any policies need improvements or elimination and work toward resolutions."

The audience applauded.

"Thank you, Carl. Now, we'll move on to the questions," Paul said. "Audience, we never reveal our questions in advance to the presidential candidates or the public.

"Carl, here's my first question. International import and export has improved drastically throughout United States history. Our economy has benefited by increased import taxes. As president, would you push for lowering or increasing our current import taxes?"

"Good question. As you mentioned, Paul, increasing our import taxes has benefited our economy. Anything that promotes production and job growth is worth continuing. Therefore, I would not recommend lowering our import taxes. These tax rates should be periodically evaluated to see if an increase is necessary."

The audience clapped in approval.

"Well done, Carl," Paul said. "Now for my next question. Same sex marriages have been legal throughout the United States for centuries now. If you were elected president, would you suggest eliminating this right?"

"The public fought for this to be passed for many years based on equality. States came on board in stages. I see no reason to discontinue something that's legal and promotes equality."

"Our viewers agree," Paul said. "Next: decades ago, all historical documents were converted from paper to electronic format. Some legislators propose that in our nearly paperless society with limited cursive writing, there is no need to retain any original historical documents. What is your take on this?"

"Well, it's true that cursive writing is rarely seen today. No one reads or writes in cursive. It disappeared in my family several generations ago. Our original documents will most likely confuse our children and future generations. They can view the documents electronically. I see no reason to keep all that ancient paper."

There was a moment of silence followed by a few clapping sounds. The audience didn't know how to respond or chose to abstain.

"This concludes tonight's show," Paul said. "Thank you and goodnight to Carl and all our viewers."

*** * ***

Dana watched Carl's show intently from home. Opponents and casual friends, they currently ranked at the top in the ratings charts. Some of their viewpoints aligned. Others conflicted. She would never consider the destruction of historical documents. Both candidates maintained impressive websites and strong social media presences. Her website was user friendly, covered hot election topics, and welcomed viewer feedback. His website was more of a reference site with no viewer interaction.

The other active New Jerseyan candidates included Julia Greene, museum curator; Ryan Davis, college professor; and Robin Tindle, civilian Army employee.

Twenty candidates entered this presidential race. Rumors suggested that several more would join. The more the merrier.

Since political parties were abolished many years ago, none of the presidential candidates had such affiliations. It was for the best as most of the candidates had mixed leanings. They would never align with the former Democratic or Republican parties.

Dana was no exception as she was as middle of the road as they come. She spent her lunch breaks and other free times campaigning in shopping centers, parks, and other public places. For the most part, the public appreciated her efforts.

Her opponents took a more distant networking approach and mailed or emailed their literature. Most recipients viewed these unsolicited mailings as junk or spam and not worth reading or keeping.

The candidates in this election didn't face the issues of their predecessors. The world was finally at peace. All nuclear weapons were destroyed years ago. The military played an active peacetime role. They volunteered their services to emergencies, communities, major events, and charities. The national deficit was long gone. Equality existed. A person's gender, race, faith, or sexual orientation was irrelevant.

Dana wouldn't be the first female president. She'd be the eleventh. Three of the previous female presidents were lesbians. Two male presidents were gay.

The presidents were United States citizens; all races were represented. Over the past several decades, the presidents' faiths included Catholic, Jewish, Protestant, Episcopalian and Latter-day Saints.

Candidates need no longer be wealthy, either. They didn't have a political party to help promote them nor were the funds needed to maintain such a party. Political parties incurred event, travel, advertising, rent–all types of expenses. The elimination of political parties also eliminated lobbyists, large campaign donations, special favors, and the like. Volunteers freely offered their support to candidates.

Poor, middle class, or wealthy, each candidate was granted equal free broadcast time and chose her or his social media participation. Presidents, vice presidents, house representatives, and senators were limited to a single five-year term. While in office, they covered all their personal expenses including, but not limited to: health care, vacations, clothing, hobbies, and other leisure activities. All job-related expenses were covered.

When elected officials left their posts, their income, round-the-clock security surveillance, covered travel, and housing ceased. They simply returned to their former lives as private citizens.

The world at peace, a healthy economy, no national deficit, and excellent, affordable health care and education–does the United States of America really need a president? Despite all the government streamlining, there has always been a president and vice president. In the current election, the new president's focus would be to maintain the current standard of living and promote improvements.

*** * ***

Dana was in her law office, typing feverishly on her computer. An intern named Evan saw her open door and tapped softly on the door frame.

"Hi, Evan. How are you?"

"Fine, Dana. Your show was great the other night. Did you select your running mate yet?"

"No, not yet. The person I had in mind is running against me." She laughed. "Carl and his running mate, Ned Swanson, are also my friends. It really is a small world. I'll find someone soon. In the meantime, my cases await."

"Understood. Let me know if I can help."

"Sure thing. Thanks, Evan."

Who would be my best running mate?

Jim Henderson was honored to join Dana's campaign. In the last election, he ran as Matt Wright's running mate. They lost by minimal votes and learned a lot in the process. Jim supported Dana's platform one hundred percent.

*** * ***

Focus TV stations throughout the United States continued broadcasting presidential candidate shows. The candidates claimed agreement on the most critical topics such as equality, health care, government term limits, strong economy, and world peace.

Truth be told, however, numerous variances surfaced. Several candidates, for example, proposed nationwide elimination of cursive writing, spelling, the arts, and numerous other subjects throughout the school systems. They also saw no reason to keep the United States' original founding documents for posterity. "Why keep paper documents?" some asked. As the campaign progressed, many candidates issued conflicting statements when questioned on equality and health care.

*** * ***

California Focus TV, Los Angeles, California

"Five ... Four ...Three ... Two ... One ...And we're on the air."

"Welcome, ladies and gentlemen. I'm Brad Parks, hosting this California Focus TV live broadcast. Our guest tonight is Jeremy Walker, a new United States of America presidential candidate. Jeremy, if you're ready, we'll begin. Please fill us in on your background."

"Hello, Brad, ladies and gentlemen," Jeremy said. "My name is Jeremy Walker and I'm running for the office of president of the United States. I'm a lifetime resident of Los Angeles, schooled in the Arts, and a longtime member of the Actors' Guild. Some of you may remember me from my five movies and various TV sitcoms.

"I come to you as a concerned citizen who wants to do great things for our country. If I was elected president, I would put my acting career aside and focus full-time on my presidential duties. Looking back through ancient United States' history, we had numerous former actors serve political offices, including presidents. I would be honored to fulfill this role."

Cheers could be heard from the audience.

"Thank you, Jeremy, Brad said. "I have a list of randomly selected questions for you. We'll get started and go through as many as possible.

"Question One. What is your stance on our current term limits for the president, house, and senate? Should we maintain or change our current term limits?"

"Excellent question. Our current term limits were imposed many years ago and should be updated. I propose increasing term limits for the president, house, and senate."

Silence prevailed throughout the audience. Many in attendance, however, submitted electronic comments to the host.

"My second question," Brad said, "concerns post-term benefits received by our president, senators, and house representatives. Should we maintain or change these benefits?"

"I view our current post-term benefits as archaic and in need of upgrading. The people who fill these government roles deserve better benefits during and after their served terms."

Audience electronic comments continued to pour in. It wasn't Questions and Answers time and Jeremy's responses were not well received by the in-house viewers. The crowd monitors were doing their best to maintain order in the audience.

They asked several viewers to leave. "Out of respect to our guest and the show's timeslot, please hold all questions and comments until the Q and A portion at the end of the show," the monitors said softly to the in-house viewers. "Remember, millions of people from all over the world are watching or recording this live show. Please be respectful and refrain from talking or other negative behavior. You're entitled to your opinions but must honor your signed agreement as a member of our live audience. If you cannot do this, please leave immediately."

"Question Three," Brad said. "Scandinavian and other European countries have experienced great success with their parental infant care leaves. Parents would alternate taking paid leaves from their jobs. The length and number of leaves varied amongst employers. For the most part, a newborn would receive parental care from birth until beginning school. Would you support such a program in the United States?"

"I've heard that some other countries have a better work-family ratio than the United States. If I was elected president, I would be interested in learning more about their successful programs. One drawback I see with giving employees more paid leave is productivity. We can't forget the employer's bottom line."

The camera crew focused only on the stage while replacements filled the empty audience seats.

Brad remained composed and smiled.

Isn't he aware of the known benefits of good work-family ratios?

"This takes us to my fourth and final question," Brad said. "United States' schools discontinued subjects such as cursive writing, phonics, spelling, home economics, music, and art nationwide. Academia, parents, and students have joined efforts to re-introduce these subjects in our schools. What is your take on this issue?"

"It's difficult for me to relate to this issue," Jeremy said. "My schools didn't offer any of these subjects. I earned my Fine Arts degrees without them. I see no purpose for phonics, spelling, or cursive writing. Some students might benefit from home economics, art, or music. I guess it depends on the students' ages and interests."

"Do you agree with reinstating *any* of these subjects?" Brad asked.

"Perhaps but not cursive writing, phonics, or spelling. I see absolutely no reason to teach these subjects."

Brad simply smiled at the audience.

At least I can sign my name and read historical documents and spell on my own.

Electronic comments from the live and remote audiences were clogging the station's inbox. The show was already running behind. The dwindled live audience appeared angry. There wasn't enough time for the staff to filter the questions and comments. Yes, they could air negative remarks about the guest's policies, but not about the guest.

"Ladies and gentlemen," Brad said, "I'm afraid we've run out of time. Your questions and comments are still pouring in and we will pass them on to our guest. I'd like to thank Jeremy and our studio audience for joining us tonight as well as all our viewers out there. Good-night, good morning, good afternoon."

Jeremy turned quickly and walked confidently off the stage. A man on a mission, he avoided all eye contact. He felt good about tonight's show and grateful to have it behind him. There'd be time for press releases and photo shoots later.

Messages to me are pouring in from all over the world. They must love me. I can't wait to read all my fan mail ...

California Focus TV continued receiving emails regarding all their Californian presidential candidate guests, especially Jeremy Walker. He was devastated when he discovered his low approval ratings following his TV appearance.

I thought I was on target. Social media, keeping fit, sharp dresser ... Those questions were controversial. I should've asked for different ones. After this blows over, I'll do another show. In the meantime, I'll build up my fan club– before it's too late.

A few new hopefuls drifted in and out of this presidential race. Three females and two males were going strong. Dana and Carl were from New Jersey. The remaining three candidates hailed from Michigan, Florida, and Vermont. As the election day drew closer, only two candidates remained standing, Dana Nelsen and Carl Thompson. They campaigned non-stop until the eleventh hour. No mud-slinging or public defamations of character. Just public speaking, social media, and literature distributions.

*** * ***

You must give the people what they want, and so Dana Nelsen did. She won the election by a landslide.

"Congratulations, Dana," Carl Thompson said over the phone. "Let me know if I can assist you with any of your upcoming challenges."

"Thanks, Carl. Our paths will surely cross again."

Dana and running mate, Jim celebrated with friends and family into the wee hours of the morning. The campaign was over. It was time for a brief period of rest and relaxation.

Two weeks later, on Inauguration Day, Jim Henderson and Dana Nelsen were officially sworn in to the offices of Vice President and President of the United States of America respectively.

Jim's office was in the White House and he moved to the official vice-presidential residence, Number One Observatory Circle, Washington, D.C. Dana enjoyed settling into her new address, 1600 Pennsylvania Ave NW, Washington, DC.

President Dana Nelsen's professional background, diligence, and ethics helped her achieve this role. May her country now stand behind her and God guide her through the challenges ahead.

Timeless

Anytown, U.S.A.

Imagine being offered the chance to enter a new dimension for a trial period. Your physical age and past is no longer relevant. All memories of your former existence are temporarily erased.

At the end of the trial period, you will decide whether to continue your new lifestyle or return to your former life. The choice will be entirely up to you. If you prefer your new norm, all memories of your former life will be permanently erased. You will only be cognizant of your current reality. On the other hand, should you decide to return to your former life, you will return to the point in time when you began this trial and resume your old life without skipping a beat.

It is natural to be skeptical of such a change or fearful of the unknown. Still, how would one know which life is better without trying both, without being open to change? You accept the trial run and feel confident that you will make the right decisions.

Despite the drastic changes in your life, you only recognize the present. Dates are tracked by calendars. Weddings, births, deaths, and any legal transactions follow a standard calendar. Dates and times are recorded for official records.

People meet their tax filing deadlines. Everything else is flexible. This eliminates the need for clocks, watches, wake up calls and alarms. Who cares what time it is? Time is irrelevant.

What does this mean besides serious problems for the clock and watch manufacturers? Tasks can be done without fear of being late. There is no need to rush about. Each moment in time is as significant as the next or the previous moment. Time is considered precious, a gift not to be wasted. Be in the moment.

Your typical *day* goes as follows. You rise in daylight, shower and dress, eat breakfast, and go on with your day. Workers and students may work on-site or from home. Others do their chores, run errands, and socialize. Individuals may fit one or more of these roles. As darkness approaches, people wind down and prepare for sleep. And so, the routine cycle continues…

Without accountable time, how do people maintain schedules? The four seasons, winter, spring, summer, and fall, guide everyone's activities. The seasons determine how we dress, which foods we grow and eat, and the activities that fit the climates.

You may like having all your routine medical checkups during one season. Someone else may prefer to scatter their medical visits throughout the year. When the time is right, you go to the appropriate health care professional. If the waiting room is crowded, you may elect to go a different day.

Most people barter for services rendered. You may prepare your doctor's taxes or give your dentist a haircut in exchange for medical services. There is no nitpicking over fair trade. All services are equally important. People are very pleasant and content. They are not stressed out or uptight.

Since there is no *time*, there are no time payments or credit purchases. People have responsibilities and they meet them. There are no debts, loans, collections, bankruptcies, or foreclosures. Everyone lives debt free with no financial worries.

How about government—is there a government? There is a very minimalist one. The President is voted in. The election is also simplified and frugal. Candidates utilize social media and free public TV as opposed to running billion-dollar campaigns.

The President serves a single five-year term. The Vice President fills in temporarily should the President be injured, ill, or otherwise unable to perform his or her duties. Should the President die, the Vice President would be in charge until a new president is elected.

The President has a small cabinet of assistants who serve as subject matter experts (SMEs) in defense, fair trade, judicial, and so forth. No special treatment is given to anyone. President and staff are paid salaries out of which they cover their own health insurance and other personal expenses. They have term limits. Once out of office, they return to their normal lives. Salaries and perks received while in office cease upon the end of their service.

The only reason the United States even needs this minimal government is because some countries still have governments. As a global leader, the United States needs representation. Americans still need some sense of protection.

Rule wise, people abide by common courtesy. Each state has law enforcement; it's quite scaled down from earlier days. Precincts exist on an as needed basis. Major cities have the largest number, while rural and suburban areas have less. Crime is at the lowest rate in U.S. history. For the most part, people who refuse to abide by common practices, leave the country.

*** * ***

My name is Liam Clarke and here is my story. I am a thirty-five-year-old American male of Irish-Italian descent. My profession is accounting. I'm a CPA with Smyth & Klein Associates, and I live and work in Bernardsville, New Jersey.

Like most New Jerseyans in my age bracket, I have accumulated debts. Between my student loans, maxed out credit cards, a hefty mortgage, property taxes, car payment, and the associated insurance payments, it's a wonder I eat.

Every day is a repeat of the previous day. I work incessantly just to pay my bills and stay afloat. Savings is negligent to non-existent. At the end of each month, I have nothing to show for my untiring efforts besides things. Just things …

Why do I have all these things? How does one deal with all their stuff? From a very early age, we learn through advertising and word of mouth about all the *things* we must have. Manufacturers and service providers do their best to convince us that we cannot survive without their products and services.

Shouldn't we be able to ascertain our own needs? Of course, there will always be extra things that we might like to have but don't really need. Advertisers erase the fine line between these *nice to haves* and *absolute needs*. All things are needed to fit in with society.

So, we "keep up with the Joneses." We measure our success by our so-called assets. But are these things really assets? Typically, anything that doesn't create income is considered a deficit. Loan (e.g., mortgage, credit card, auto) interest payments are not assets. Income properties, savings, dividends, and wise investments are examples of prospective assets.

The bottom line is: I'm essentially drowning in debt. I've acquired a lot of stuff, none of which are true assets. My debts exceed my assets.

*** * ***

Today, I was sitting on a bench outside my office building, when a man sat down beside me.

"Hello, Liam," he said.

I turned to him, and said, "Hello. Have we met?"
"Indirectly," he said. "I know that you're a top-notch accountant with Smyth & Klein. You're living the *good life* in this beautiful town. Despite your envious lifestyle, you're looking for a change. That's where I come in."

"Go on."

"I am offering you an opportunity to live a much simpler life for a two-week trial period. Should you accept this offer, the transition will be seamless. Time will be frozen during your absence. You'll be transferred there directly.

"At the end of the trial, you'll decide whether to stay or return here. If you stay, all memories of your present life will be erased. On the other hand, if you choose to return here, you'll lose all memory of your trial experience."

"Wow, this sounds like a Twilight Zone adventure. You said this trial life is simpler. Please explain."

"Simpler lifestyle ... We don't all agree on what this entails. The only way for you to decide if this simpler life is for you, is to experience it. Should you take the challenge, you'll be briefed with the necessary background information. You'll remain an accountant, have an office, and a furnished apartment."

"I see... Tell me though, if I decide to go to this mysterious place and participate in this unusual trial life, how will I get there? What's the weather forecast? I have no idea what to pack. If I want to return to my current life, how will I get back? Can you guarantee my safe transports to and from?"

"So many questions and concerns, my friend... You're not alone. I hear these same questions, again and again. We all have dreams and goals. Some of us are more open to change than others. Often, the familiar norm is followed out of fear of the unknown.

"Should you accept this offer, you'll be transported there. You'll have all the necessary clothing and incidentals for the trial. At the end of the trial period, should you choose to come back, you'll be transported here."

"So then, I don't need to pack a thing. How about my employer and creditors? Don't I need to tell *anyone* my whereabouts?"

"Liam, remember, this is a two-week trial for *you*. Time here will be frozen for the next two weeks. Should you return, you'll walk back into your current office, as if you just finished this lunch break. If you stay on, you'll begin a new slate with no memories of this life. You'll become a distant memory to all the people you currently know. You risk *nothing* by doing this trial."

"The permanent decision will be much tougher. I'll need to be sure that I *never* want to return. How do I know that I can trust all your promises of transports, housing, and a job?"

"I guess this qualifies as a *Leap of Faith*."

"When must I respond?"

"I can give you some time alone. Finish your lunch. Think it over. I'll return shortly."

The stranger quickly walked off and left me with my thoughts.

The truth is, I have no one significant in my life. Sure, I have surface level friends, business associates and neighbors, and a pile of creditors. My parents passed years ago ... no siblings, wife or even a steady girlfriend ... What's keeping me here? Besides, it's only a trial ...

*** * ***

I approach this trial lifestyle change with caution and exhilaration. My transport here was seamless and quick. No suitcases or car at my disposal, and yet, I have everything I need.

Well, it's day one. I think it's still okay to use a date reference. If I stay here long enough, I wonder if I'll still know the date. Not setting an alarm clock sounds nice. Of course, I don't really need an alarm clock. I'm an accountant after all. Accountants must be organized. I believe that we all have our own inner body clock.

I have a temporary apartment and office for the next two weeks. No need to wear a watch here. I keep checking my bare left wrist. No one here seems concerned about the time.

The adults here are employed or retired and do their own thing. I'm still an accountant. No need for designer suits here. If I decide to stay on, I'll only need a few suits for special occasions.

*** * ***

Day one

My first day proved to be quite interesting. A gentleman named Joe appeared in my office this morning around nine or ten. It's easy to lose track of time around here. We're about the same age. He's fit, pragmatic, and friendly, and he owns the local barber shop. His shop is the old-fashioned type with a pole out front. I may prepare his taxes in exchange for a year's worth of haircuts.

Eddie, a licensed electrician in his forties, arrived next. He offered his electrical services as payment for my financial advice. Cool.

A middle-aged man named Frank stopped by. He's the town butcher, and he only sells meat from local free-range animals. No antibiotics, genetically modified organisms, (GMOs), or fillers are used.

Sam, a strapping young train conductor, visited and offered me discounts on train tickets for financial advice.

Later that evening, I had a brief conversation with my landlord. He needs a personal and business accountant. I'm qualified for both roles. He suggested negotiating a rental deal. I can't even imagine doing this with my previous landlords.

I tracked all my business discussions on a notepad. Old habits, I guess. I'm new to this timeless environment.

*** * ***

My day one clients and I will probably use the barter system. How will I survive here with no income? Of course, I'll earn some money. It's not feasible that all my clients will barter. Bartering versus debits and credits is so new to me.

Another strange thing–I haven't needed to drive since arriving. People drive occasionally here but not like back home. Why do I keep thinking about *back home*? I guess this is all so new. I reach for my car keys and realize that I don't have a car nor do I need one here.

Around town ...

The local grocery store is a one-stop indoor farmers market that also sells paper and soap products. Unlike traditional supermarkets, the local farmers tend their stands. They sell fresh in season fruits, vegetables, and dairy products, including home-made ice creams.

Frank, the town butcher, mans the meat display. His refrigerated display case contains an assortment of fresh meats. Customers order ahead or in person. The local baker, Jim, is another regular merchant. He sells a wide assortment of cakes, cookies, pies, and breads; he also fills custom orders.

All the businesses within this quaint town are tightly clustered and easily accessible to the residents on foot. The grocery store limits its merchandise to foods, and household paper and soap products. Imagine—one grocery store supports the local farmers, butcher, and baker instead of major food and household retailers.

Everything else is covered by the remaining local merchants. If you want a book, magazine, or writing materials, you go to the nearby book store. The drug store sells all prescription and over the counter medicines and health care products. A party shop is filled with greeting cards, wrappings, decorations, and party supplies.

Strange? Wouldn't customers prefer one-stop shopping? Why not purchase lawn chairs, have tires installed on your car, and buy liquor for your party where you shop for groceries? This is how our huge shopping malls and discount centers are replacing our individual Ma and Pa businesses. The butcher, the baker, the candlestick maker ...

Remember women's dress boutiques, men's haberdashers, and hat shops for both genders? How about shoe repair or cobbler shops? It may sound convenient to do all shopping under one roof. Huge stores, however, can be overwhelming. No seller can be an expert in all types of merchandise. A seller's ability to place bulk orders doesn't guarantee all quality products and services. Wouldn't it make sense to support multiple merchants who specialize in their products and are passionate about what they do? Think about it …

Some might see the previously described scenario as a monopoly. One grocer, one butcher, one baker—what, no competition? Competition has never been outlawed in this town; it just hasn't been needed.

Why? One business example is Sara's Dress Boutique. Sara has been into fashion since grade school. Her degree in fashion design is from one of the best fashion schools in the world. One might expect her to mark up her merchandise but she doesn't. The local merchants offer no competition, but the Internet does, and so do the nearby town merchants. If she continues to provide her customers with personal attention and quality merchandise at a fair price, why would they go elsewhere?

*** * ***

Early one work morning …

I gathered my dirty laundry and stopped in the town laundromat. A petite, dark-haired woman appeared from the back of the shop. "Hi. I'm Monica," she said. "Good timing. Lots of open machines."

"Hello, Monica. I'm Liam. I moved here recently, still finding my way around."

"Welcome. What type of work do you do?"

"Accounting. My office is next to the bank."

"Accounting? That's great. I, for one, could use your help with my taxes. Will you be doing laundry or dropping off?"

"You offer a drop-off service?"

"Sure do. Folks use it now and then. I wash, dry, and fold their laundry for a small fee. Sometimes we barter."

"Nice. For now, I'll do my own. Do you have a bill changer?"

"Uh-huh, near the folding tables." She directed me there. "The vending machine has laundry products."

"I brought my own but good to know."

"Well, I'll leave you to your laundry then. I'll be in the back room, if you need anything." She smiled warmly.

She's something else. This whole town is. Between this place and the dry cleaners, I'm set for now. No sense buying a washer and dryer.

I made a quick stop at my place with my newly-cleaned laundry. Then I headed directly to Tina and Tom's Dry Cleaners.

As I entered the shop, a woman behind the counter smiled at me. "Hello," she said. "I'm Tina. May I help you?"

"Hi. I'm Liam, and I need a few things dry cleaned."

"Oh, Liam, you must be our resident accountant; Welcome."

"That's me. Nice to meet you."

"Well, how are we doing? Do you like our little town and the people so far?"

"Great. This place is like no other. My travels have taken me to major cities, open countrysides, and suburbs, but I've *never* experienced a place like this. Everyone is so friendly and open here. This town is like a well-oiled machine. You support each other as a team instead of destroying each other's dreams as competitors."

"You're a quick learner, Liam. That sums up our town. I hope you enjoy living here. Now ...what are we doing with these dress shirts? Do you prefer hangers or boxes? I don't recommend starch for this fabric."

"Hangers and no starch, please."

"These will be ready tomorrow," Tina said as she handed me a claim ticket.

"Anytime tomorrow?"

"Anytime between daybreak and dusk."

"Thanks, Tina. Have a nice day." I smiled and headed to work.

*** * ***

As I walked down the hall to my office, I noticed a small, silver-haired man inserting mail in the named slots on the wall.

"Hello," I said. "You must be our mail carrier."

"That's right. I'm Harry, and you are?"

"Liam. I'm the new accountant. I doubt if you have any mail for me."

"Liam, hmmm ... sounds familiar. Yup, you've got mail."

"I do? Don't tell me all those junk mailers found me already."

"I'm not familiar with *junk* mail. We enjoy getting mail. Important papers, personal correspondence, and packages. Here's what I have for you today." He handed me a thick stack of envelopes.

"Thanks, Harry. Nice meeting you."

"Welcome, Liam; good day."

I stared in amazement at my overflowing stack of mail. I've been here less than a week. Are my old creditors coming after me? How could they without a forwarding address? *I* don't even know my new address. Besides, this deal included no past liabilities.

I dropped the mail on my desk and closed my office door. May as well at least sort this heap and start going through it.

The envelopes were standard white and assorted colors and sizes. I started with a small, pink envelope. Inside was a welcome card from Sara, the dress boutique owner. A standard size white envelope contained a welcome note from Eddie, the electrician. Joe, the town barber, sent a friendly note in a blue envelope.

All the envelopes contained cheery greetings from the townspeople. Some also asked me to contact them to schedule an appointment. I already met some of them and looked forward to meeting the rest.

Not a single bill or piece of junk mail … I wasn't expecting any bills at this point seeing as I haven't made any credit card purchases. I've covered all my expenses here to date with cash or barter. A town without junk mail—now that's amazing …

I continued going through all my mail and made a separate pile of the appointment requests. Then I came up with a tentative schedule. I'd begin with barber, Joe and see as many folks as possible over the next several days.

*** * ***

Visiting clients

Joe's barber shop was vintage. I especially liked the barber poll out front. As my feet touched the creaky, hardwood floor of the shop, I envisioned the barber shops of yesteryears. Joe recreated this essence throughout. The barber chairs, hot-towel shaves, razors, and waiting chairs with magazines reminded me of my grandfather's stories and classic movies.

"Liam, good to see you again," Joe said.

"Hi, Joe. Got your note and thought I'd stop by. Is this a good time?"

"Sure, no clients now. Need a trim or a shave?"

"Not today, thanks. Great shop—so retro."

"Thanks, I wanted the real deal."

"And you got it. So, when should we meet?"

"Does lunch, tomorrow work? I'll bring lunch; we can talk and eat."

"Sounds great." I jotted down the appointment on my notepad. "See you tomorrow."

I guess lunch time is noonish or when folks' stomachs grumble …

Next, I stopped at the bakery shop. Bells rang cheerfully as I opened the front door.

A man greeted me from behind the counter. "Hello," he said. "I'm Jim. May I help you?"

"Hi, Jim. I'm Liam, the accountant. Thanks for your note."

"Welcome, Liam. I'm glad you stopped in. I need to schedule some time with you. Are you free tomorrow morning? If so, once the early birds leave, I'll stop by with coffee and donuts."

"Works for me." I added Jim's appointment to my notepad.

Clients who come bearing gifts—who would've thought?

"Speaking of donuts," Jim said, "I just filled the front case from the cooling racks and brewed coffee. Can I get you anything?"

"Everything looks and smells amazing. Coffee black and a chocolate cruller, please."

I enjoyed my coffee and donut on a bench across the street. Next stop, Sara's dress boutique. Her storefront was inviting. The colorful window display was filled with beautiful clothes and accessories. As I entered her shop, I heard classical music playing softly in the background. Splendid hardwood flooring and area rugs blended well with the color coordinated furnishings, and wall hangings. A light floral scent permeated the room.

A young woman with strawberry blonde hair was folding garments on a display table. She looked up and smiled at me. "Hi, I'm Sara," she said. "May I help you?"

"Nice meeting you, Sara. I'm Liam. Thanks for your note. I stopped by to say 'Hi.' Your shop is beautiful."

And so are you …

"Thanks, Liam. I keep up with the latest fashions, and the ladies really enjoy shopping here. Please send your wife or girlfriend my way. I'll take good care of her."

"I currently have no lady in my life, but when I need a lady's gift, I'll definitely see you."

Sara blushed. "Please do … and I need to see you about my accounting."

"Sure, when's good for you?" I asked.

"How's next Monday late morning sound? I'll open up and stop by during a lull time."

I added Sara's appointment to my notebook. "Perfect."

"See you Monday, Liam." She smiled warmly.

Am I imagining things or did she just wink at me? Beauty, brains, and so nice.

*** * ***

I stopped at the cinema to see the owner, Jenny. People rushed by me, anxious to purchase tickets and refreshments. When I approached the counter, I spotted a woman wearing a name tag that resembled a movie director's clapboard and displayed, "Director, Jenny."

"Hi, Jenny. My name is Liam. I'm the new accountant you contacted. I appreciate your nice card."

"Liam, yes, welcome to my cinema. Would you like to see a movie? Our schedule is on the board in the lobby. A few favorites are about to start."

"No, some other time. I just stopped by to introduce myself and ask when you'd like to meet."

"Oh, good, let me get my schedule." She disappeared somewhere behind the counter.

"What kind of popcorn do you sell?" I asked a female concessions clerk.

"Organic, air popped. No oils or GMOs–just a little salt. Here's a taste." She filled a container with popped kernels and handed it to me with a broad smile.

"Ummh, thank you. This tastes even better than it smells."

With that, Jenny reappeared with a small notebook and pen. "Where does time go?" she asked. "Sorry, fully booked—can I get back to you?"

"Sure, I'll note a reminder."

"You, too?" She asked and laughed out loud. "Everyone teases me about my notetaking, but it helps me remember important things."

"I know," I said. "Prior to moving here, between electronics and sticky notes, I had non-stop reminders. When folks started asking to see me, I started a notepad—beats sticky notes."

"Sticky notes must be new. I've been here a long time."

"How long?"

"Good question since we're timeless. I don't recall my previous life."

"None of it?"

"I used to get occasional flashbacks—maybe they were dreams."

"Interesting... Well, Jenny, good night. See you when you're ready."

She smiled with her eyes and ran off to assist an employee.

I stepped outside just in time to catch a beautiful sunset. The sky had a pinkish hue.

Beautiful people here, inside and out. Red sky at night, sailor's delight ...

The blazing sun slowly eased out of view. Time for all day workers to head home or out to dinner. It had been an interesting, busy day and I needed to just go home and chill.

The following morning ...

I arrived at my office bright and early. Jim was due in once his early crowd left. I grabbed a legal pad and pens and cleared a good working space on my desk. I had a good view of the town from my office window, and sure enough, Jim was carrying a box and heading my way.

Coffee and donuts?

"Good morning, Jim," I said. "Come in, take a seat."

"Good morning, Liam. As promised, coffee, and the donuts are fresh off the cooling rack."

"Everything smells incredible. Chocolate crullers– you remembered."

"Sure, they're airy; we can eat more."

"And we do. Now, how can I help you?" I asked.

"A couple of things," Jim said. "I keep good business records, do my own taxes, and keep up with my bills. Plus, I'm working on my savings.

"Baking is my life. I'm third generation in the business. When it comes to finances, though, I'm no expert. I don't take business courses or follow the tax laws and deductions. You have this expertise. I need a business plan, you know … expansion and retirement planning."

"That's right up my alley. Did you bring any business records?"

"No, I wanted to see if you were on board, and if so, get a list of what you need from me."

I quickly wrote a list on my legal pad and handed the sheet to Jim. "Here's a list of what I'll need to get started. Let me know when you're ready. Once I begin, I'll let you know if I need anything else."

"I should have all this together in no time. As for your fees, do you have an estimate for all this?"

"Once I review your records, I'll have a better idea of what you need. Then we'll meet to discuss everything."

"Sounds good, my friend. I'll be back with your wish list."

"I'll be here. Thanks for breakfast; it hit the spot."

"Anytime."

I walked Jim out and checked my mail slot. Harry must've been here. I reached in and grabbed a stack of envelopes. One by one, I opened each one. They all contained welcome messages. I also received new appointment requests. Once again, I separated the stacks and added the new meeting requests to my schedule.

*** * ***

Time flew by as always. I was deeply engrossed in one of my financial reference books, when I heard a tapping sound. I looked up and saw Joe, the barber, with lunch for the two of us.

I jumped up from my seat, and said, "Hi, Joe. How are you? Whatever that is smells great."

"Hi, Liam. I forgot to ask about food allergies. Meatball subs, Tony's special today."

"Great choice. No known allergies and I like everything. Thanks so much. Make yourself at home. I'll grab some napkins. Coffee, water?"

"Black coffee, please."

"Two black coffees and napkins coming right up."

You'd think we were teenagers the way we devoured our hot sandwiches. They fit the criteria of three-napkin meals.

"That was a close tie to my Italian mother's meatballs," I said.

"Yeah, 'ole Tony sure knows his way 'round the kitchen. Met him yet?"

"No, but I will soon. Now, what can I do for you?"

"Well, as you know, I'm the only barber in town. The guys could cut their own hair or go to nearby towns, but they remain loyal. Even the bald guys enjoy an occasional shave. I must be doing something right."

"Your shop is amazing. I've only seen similar in classic movies and photos."

"Good to hear, especially from a newcomer. Believe it or not, I've never had a business accountant. I'd like your feedback on my bookkeeping."

"Do you have debt or credit problems?"

"No, my business and personal bills are current. No outstanding debts, liens, or other issues."

"Do you have plans to renovate or open a second location?"

"Not really–at least not now. We support each other here instead of competing. If a new barber wanted to open a shop, we'd work together and share expenses. Heck, I could use a backup when I need time off. So far, I'm *it* in the barber business."

"Uh-huh, I see the norm here—one barber, one baker, one dress shop, and so forth. This is a small town when compared to a large, heavily populated city. The smallness offers more diverse interests and closeness amongst the residents."

"I think you're right," Joe said. "A huge city could have a deli or barber on every corner with constant competition and price wars."

"Getting back to your books, did you bring any records today?"

"No, I wasn't sure what you'd need."

I wrote a list of financial records and handed it to Joe. "This should do for starters. I'll go through them and we can meet again to discuss next steps. You may not need to change a thing. I may have some suggestions for now or later."

"I'll get to this right away. Should we discuss fees or bartering?"

"I've yet to see any business fees here. What do you say I go over your records and we come up with an agreement?"

"Sounds like a plan," Joe said.

"Oh, and thanks again for lunch. I'm stuffed."

"I hear you; I feel a nap coming on."

Joe was my last appointment of the day and I needed to walk off my high carb breakfast and lunch. I figured Frank, the butcher, would be working in his shop or at his grocery store stand. I found him in his shop. He was waiting on a customer. Sawdust covered creaky floors and a retro wooden pickle barrel near the counter caught my eye.

I hadn't seen a shop like this since my childhood days. I often accompanied my mother on errand runs. Our local butcher always treated me to one of his homemade garlic pickles which I immediately devoured. This apparently drew a crowd of onlookers every time.

After Frank's customer left, I approached his counter. "Welcome, Liam," Frank said.

"Hi, Frank. I love what you've done with your shop. The great pickle barrel and sawdust especially bring back fond childhood memories."

"Please, help yourself. I've always loved these old barrels and pickles."

"Don't mind if I do." I selected a small pickle from the barrel and ate it quickly. "Mmm, this is so fresh," I said.

"What can I get you? Lots of specials today."

"Nothing today, thanks. I stocked up at the grocery store. I received your note. Do you want to meet?"

"Sure. I'll collect my business records and bring food for us. I'll make something or stop by Tony's. Have you tried his deli yet?"

""Just once. I had his meatball sub today."

"The best around," Frank said. "Any food allergies?"

"No, thankfully. See you soon."

*** * ***

Speaking of Tony and his meatball sub, I headed toward his shop next. As I stepped inside the deli, I breathed in peppers and onions on the grill, pasta salads, and an array of lunch meats and cheeses. A man was rearranging some platters in the display case.

He looked up and said, "Hi. I'm Tony. New to town?"

"Yes, I'm Liam, the new accountant."

Tony removed his disposable gloves, walked around the counter, and shook my hand.

"Liam, welcome. Hungry? I've got hot food, cold sandwiches, salads, snacks, and cold drinks."

"Not now, thanks. A client brought your meatball subs for lunch … just like my mom's, God rest her soul …."

"Sorry about your mom … Bet you're a big city man, too. Thanks, it's my own twist on an old family recipe. Glad you liked it."

"Liked it? I could become obese living here."

"Not you. You're fit. Besides, my food has no preservatives, fillers, trans fats, or GMOs. I buy all my meats fresh from Frank and the rest from our other grocers—all fresh and natural."

"Incredible. Say, thanks for your note. You asked about meeting?"

"Yeah, I definitely need some accounting advice. Guess you're hearing from all the other business owners too …"

"Quite a few. Everyone's going out of their way to make me feel welcome and being busy is a good thing. Can you gather your tax records for the past two years and most recent bank statement and stop by sometime?"

"Okay, I'll use a sealed envelope in case you're out."

"Sure, if I'm not in, leave it in my mail slot outside my office."

"Just a sec," Tony said. He disappeared to a back room for a few minutes and then reappeared carrying a sealed bag. "If you liked my meatball sub, you'll love my eggplant parm. I gave you the entrée this time—less bread."

"Dinner—you're the best. What do I owe you?"

"On the house. I overcooked. No sense wasting good food. You look like you could use a break."

"Thanks, see you soon."

The bag was steamy hot. Tony was right; I needed a break. It was Friday night. No more appointments until Monday morning. I headed home to unwind.

What goes on here over the weekends? I guess I'm about to find out …

I slept a little later Saturday morning without missing the sunrise. After a light breakfast and shower, I dressed for a walk into town. Some shops were open as usual, such as the bakery, grocery, and butcher. Sara's boutique window displayed the "Closed" sign. Of course, she usually opened a little later in the morning.

There was a slight chill in the air and a touch of dew on the grass and trees. I zipped up my jacket and inhaled the cool, fresh air. As I approached the local park, I noticed a few people walking their dogs and jogging. Off in the distance, near the amphitheater, a small group of people were busily unpacking some storage containers. I headed over to them.

"Hi," I said. "My name is Liam; I'm a newcomer. Is there a performance here today?"

One young man in the group said, "Hi, Liam. I'm Elliott. We're just setting up the stage for today's Theatre in the Park performances."

"Really? How often do you have these plays?"

"Every Saturday, weather permitting. People usually show up around lunch time. We do one or two performances based on how we're feeling and the crowds."

"That's great. What's on for today?"

"Fiddler on the Roof."

"Aha, one of my all-time favorites. I wouldn't miss it. Can I help you with anything?"

"Why, sure, we could use a hand setting up the sound equipment, chairs, and things."

"Lead the way," I said.

The stage and seating area was ready to go in no time. I bid my new friends farewell and continued my walk around the park.

Why not make the most of this beautiful free day? I'll grab a coffee and circle back close to lunch time. I vaguely recall some outdoor plays from my past. They weren't offered regularly, however, and I usually missed seeing them. Elliott said that all performances are free. If the actors won't accept donations, I'll offer my time.

I leisurely circled the park and passed the playground and tennis courts. The bakery sign beckoned me.

"Jim, good morning," I said as I entered his shop. "Liam, enjoying your day off?"

"Sure, I left my apartment early this morning and just wandered around town and into the park. Met some of the theatre group; we set up for today's play."

"Great, are you catching today's show? We're so proud of our theatre group. They're very good."

"I'm heading there next. They're performing Fiddler on the Roof. Stopped for coffee and crullers."

"This tray just came out. Black coffee with a couple of chocolate ones?"

"Perfect."

In walked Sara. "Hi, there, Jim, Liam. Beautiful day, eh?"

"I'll say," I said to Sara. "Are you working today?"

Speaking of beautiful ...

"Just a little longer. I work a short day most Saturdays and close Sundays. Sometimes, I take a long weekend."

"That's good," I said. "We all need time off now and then."

"Jim," she said, "I'd like an iced coffee and a slice of your scrumptious apple nut cake, please."

"Coming right up," Jim said.

"Mmm, that sounds delicious; I'll try it next time."

"Everything in here is delicious—all in moderation," she said. "Remember, I have all sorts of beautiful things for your ladies. Have a wonderful day, gentlemen." She flashed her most contagious smile. Her dress heels clicked as she left with her take-out. Through the front window, I glimpsed her subtle wink.

Flirting or tired eyes? No lady in my life—at least not yet...
*** * ***

As Elliott predicted, a crowd appeared. I grabbed a vacant seat and nodded to the people nearby. The performance was outstanding–Broadway outdoors. The theatre group appreciated our standing ovation. They'd take a break and return for a second show.

I approached the young man who played the part of Perchik and shook his hand.

"Very well done, young man," I said.

"Why thank you, sir," he replied while remaining in character.

"Trust me, I've seen many plays, on and off Broadway. Your theatre group is one of the finest around."

"Many thanks again, sir. I'll be sure to tell the others."

"Is your group from all over, or do you all live here?"

"We're all locals with a passion for the theatre. Our regular performances give us plenty of stage time. We support each other no matter what."

"Unlike typical competitive, back-stabbing performers."

"Exactly."

"Refreshing to hear. You'd best relax and save your voice and energy," I said. "Good luck to you. I'll see you here again soon."

"Thank you, sir, for your kind words and supporting the arts."

"Ah, yes, does your group accept donations?"

"So far, we haven't. If you'd like to help us set up again sometime, please do. The locals have donated all our costumes, props, chairs, and backdrops. We give our time and energy freely. Thanks for asking, though."

What a town this is—so many incredible people ...

I walked around town aimlessly, stopping periodically to window shop. As I was passing Sara's shop, I glanced in the front window and our eyes locked. I could feel her dimpled smile through the window.

Once inside her shop, I said, "Greetings."

She smiled warmly. "Long time no see. I'm open a few more minutes ..."

"I won't keep you … guess I lost track of the time. Just passing by, admiring your window display, and I saw your smiling face. You have a wonderful smile, by the way."

"Ahhh, thanks, Liam. I'm an optimist and usually upbeat."

"And it shows. I was wondering ... do you have any plans after closing today?"

"No, nothing definite. I guess I'll just head home for dinner; it's been hours since brunch."

"You must be starving. May I take you to dinner? Name the place."

"I'm hungry, and yes, dinner sounds nice. Do you like Chinese food? We have an excellent place in town. I'm flexible, if not."

"I love Chinese food. Need help closing?"

"No, I'm set. I'll hit the lights and lock up on our way out."

"Shall we, then?" I asked.

"After you."

Free at last, we linked arms and walked to the Chinese restaurant. Sara was right. The last time I had sesame noodles of this caliber was in my favorite Asian spot in New York City.

Sara and I took a leisurely stroll around town after dinner. You'd think we were longtime friends based on our continuous chatter and laughter. We entered the park and stopped in our tracks.

"The moon is so full," she said.

"I'll say. We don't need street lights tonight."

We took a loop around the park., talking about anything and everything. Eventually, we ended up at Sara's front door.

"Thank you, Liam." She flashed me her warmest smile. "I had a wonderful time."

"Me, too. Good company and food and lots of laughs."

"Laughing is good," she said. "I'm off tomorrow; I guess you are, too. I'm looking forward to sleeping in and catching up on house stuff, errands, and things."

"Sounds good. Force yourself to take a *me* break, too. You deserve it after working six days straight."

"Definitely. It's a lot of work running my shop alone. Long hours, skipped meals, but the weeks fly by because I love what I'm doing."

"Wise saying, '*Choose a job you love, and you will never have to work a day in your life.*' "

"I love that quote. On that note, goodnight, Liam. Have a good day tomorrow and I'll see you in your office Monday morning."

"Goodnight, Sara. Until Monday morning then."

Our first date was void of the usual uncomfortable moments. I didn't want it to end. The man in the moon guided me home.

Sunday flew by. I slept in and awoke feeling rested and famished. After polishing off a hefty brunch, I refilled my coffee mug and lost myself in a very thick novel. Later that night, I tried my best to wind down. Sleep didn't come easily. Ironic as this may sound, I didn't have much more time here. Very soon I must commit to stay or leave. I had best choose wisely as there was no turning back ...

Monday morning, while sipping coffee in my office, I pulled out a legal pad and drew a vertical line down the center of the top sheet. At the top of the page, I added a header on the left, *Stay* and on the right, *Go.*

Then I grabbed a pencil and started filling in the rows.

Thank God for erasers …

My list was slowly evolving as I added, erased, and rearranged my items. I heard a slight tapping sound and looked up to see Sara's smiling face.

"Sara, good morning," I said. I walked over to greet her.

"Hi, Liam. Can you see me now or …?"

"Of course—please come in, relax."

We got our coffees and settled in around my desk.

"So, how are things at the shop?" I asked.

"Good. I had a wedding party come in this morning. I'm dressing the bride and her attendants. We're still in the fun planning stage. Craziness comes later."

"I can only imagine."

"It's not so bad," she said. "Stress isn't bad if you don't let it get to you."

"You're right. How about the business financials? Does keeping the books increase your stress level?"

"At times, yes. I'm fine with the day to day record keeping, ordering, sales, and banking. My main business stressors are filing taxes and other government papers. I also need a solid business plan."

"This is common with small business owners like you. Running the business drains all your time and energy. How can you possibly keep up with ever-changing tax laws and future planning?"

"You've got that right. Can you help me with my taxes and financial planning?"

"Yes, definitely. When you get a chance, pull these business records together: your most recent bank statement, and all your government filings for the last two years. You can drop them off or I'll stop by." I wrote these items on a sheet of paper and handed it to her.

"Great. Thanks so much for seeing me. I need to get back to work and I'm sure you're busy too. Have a nice day." Her smile was genuine.

I walked with her into the hallway. "You, too," I said. "Don't be a stranger."

Sara was right about my workload. I was close to completing my recommendations for Joe and halfway through Eddie's file. Once I finished these two, I planned to move on to Jim's. Meanwhile, additional requests for my services appeared daily in my mail slot. As I rifled through today's mail, I opened a note from Monica, the laundromat lady. She'd be stopping by soon. I glanced out my office window and saw her heading my way.

That was fast. I should hear her footsteps shortly unless she's headed elsewhere … and here she comes …

"Greetings, Monica." I met her at my office door and ushered her inside.

"Hi, Liam," she said. "I don't have an appointment. Running errands and took a chance ..."

"Now's fine. What can I do for you?"

Monica settled into the chair across from me and smiled. "Well, I could use some help with my business accounting and taxes. I've been handling all the daily operations plus the books from day one. The last couple of years, I started stressing over my taxes, especially with all the new forms."

"Understandable. My job requires keeping up on all the tax changes. It can't be easy for business owners on tight schedules. Sure, I can go through all your books and do your filings and make suggestions. Do you have anything due soon or when would you like to get started?"

"Nothing due right now. What do you say we meet within the next three weeks? I'll pull all my records and make an appointment."

"Sounds great, Monica. You know where to find me."

"Well, okay then. I'll leave you to your work. We'll talk soon." She rose from her chair, shook my hand firmly and smiled with her eyes.

My legal pad decision list was in plain view. As thoughts came to me, I updated the two columns on my list.

I'm already committing to work beyond my trial date. If I go back, what happens to my clients? I hope my replacement treats them right. My time here is about to end, or my new life is just beginning. Which path should I take?

It would be a no-brainer if I had someone special in my life back home. The guilt of deserting my significant other, children, or other family members without even saying good-bye would kill me. Even if my entire past could be erased from my memory, what about *their* memories?

Anyway, all of this is hypothetical because sadly, I have no one waiting for me back home. No one who would seriously miss me. Perhaps that's why I couldn't refuse this trial offer. I wonder if the others here had similar situations. How many trial residents stay? How many leave?

Just two weeks ago, I was one of the most competitive accountants in prestigious Bernardsville, New Jersey. My firm was extremely cut-throat. I've witnessed none of this here. One butcher shop, one deli, one bakery … Everyone supports everyone. Why, according to Joe, should another barber want in, they'd work together and cover for each other. I can't even imagine this scenario back home. Back home? Why does *back home* no longer sound comforting?

*** * ***

I divided the remainder of my extended work day between my active files. The refreshing breezes and radiant full moon compelled me to stretch my legs. Upon entering the park, I immediately immersed myself in the earthy scents, rustling leaves, and the open sky. The Big Dipper looked close enough to touch. I couldn't recall ever seeing the constellations so clearly, especially with my naked eyes.

Walking along slowly, quickly, I just kept going with no real destination in mind. Minutes, hours, miles went by in a flash. Suddenly I realized that it was late and I still hadn't eaten. Soon it would be morning. The invisible clock was ticking. I had best complete my list ...

*** * ***

Well, today's the day. I have no idea how or where or when things will evolve, but today marks the end of my trial period here. Will the gentleman who offered me this trial or someone local pay me a personal visit or will mental telepathy be utilized?

I went to my office as usual. Jim's lights were on. Of course, he opened his bakery early every day. No signs of life yet in my building. I brewed coffee and stood looking out my office window for several minutes. Very soon, this sleepy town would be wide awake. Everyone would be out and about, working, shopping, playing, or simply relaxing.

I finished all my clients' reports and carefully sealed them in labeled envelopes. Additional work requests came in. Tony dropped off records for my review. Sara was almost ready to meet. Don't the residents know about today?

Initiating new clients' work and pouring over my mail, the hours flew by. It was suddenly lunch time, so, I grabbed take-out from Tony's and headed over to the park. I spotted an empty bench shaded by a weeping willow tree and sat down. Deep in thought, I proceeded to enjoy my lunch.

"Is this seat taken?"

I looked up at Sara's beautiful face. "It is now," I said. "How are you, Sara?"

"Fine, and you?"

"I'm doing okay. Catching up on all my clients' files."

"Busy is good. I have two wedding parties and all my regulars right now. It seems like everyone needs alterations at once. I sew, but there's only so many hours in a day. Besides, Tina's better with major alterations; she's swamped too."

"Tina, the dry cleaner? That makes sense."

"Uh-huh, we help each other out that way. Listen, I said that we'd meet soon, but things are crazy right now ... I haven't had a spare minute. Could we postpone meeting until next week?"

I looked deep into her eyes and ran my fingers through her hair. Was that a tear on her cheek? I pulled her close and hugged her tightly. "Yes, Sara, next week sounds wonderful. Take your time ..."

Turn Back Time

Greetings. My name is Daniel Adams. I'm an American male citizen currently living in Princeton, New Jersey. My foreign language and history degrees opened many interesting and challenging doors for me. Still, something was missing with each job. That was until I stumbled upon my current career path.

A young college graduate with numerous job opportunities, my life sounds promising but very ordinary. Trust me, it's far from ordinary. You see, along with my extensive language skills and love of all cultures and history is my love of travel. And travel I do, every chance I get ...

*** * ***

Berlin, Germany 1920s

In 1925, Paul von Hindenburg was elected to the powerful office of President of the Reich (*Reichspräsident*), Germany's head of state under the Weimar Republic.

Europe and the United States struggled to recover following World War I which ended in 1918. The Roaring Twenties represented a time to party and celebrate the world at peace. Lavish parties, cabarets, and night life abound. The music, dancing, films, and shows of the time were mostly frivolous.

Then the Wall Street stock market crashed on October 29, 1929. The United States experienced the initial devastating impact. The economic downfall quickly spread globally.

Prohibition set in. People everywhere were suddenly jobless, penniless with little or no means of survival. They stood in long bread lines hoping to walk away with bread or other rationed handouts for their families. Banks and governments could not grant or accept loans. Each country needed to focus first on recovering from within.

Berlin, Germany was not exempt from the economic downfall. Prostitution was on the rise. Many women chose this route to survive. Later, youths of both genders joined them. The entertainment industry in general was becoming more liberal worldwide. Too liberal, too quickly for the majority to comprehend and embrace. Businesses were folding. In the northern industrial areas, the unemployment rate reached seventy percent. The nation was hungry, depressed, and frightened.

*** * ***

Today I received an opportunity of a lifetime. My mission, should I choose to accept it, is to enter this extremely stressful point in history. A successful mission will positively alter the course of history throughout the world. How could I possibly refuse? This exciting challenge is set to begin with President Paul von Hindenburg's New Year's Eve Gala. It's time to prepare, to immerse my very being in Germany, 1929.

Tuesday, December 31, 1929, Berlin, Germany

My mission packet, complete with new identity, travel documents, bank accounts, and foreign currency is in order. Hello. My name is Edmund Schmidt.

I've had mixed feelings about accepting this mission. Passing apprehension, naturally. Still, there was no way that I could decline this opportunity of a lifetime.

As I approached the historic Brandenburg Gate (Brandenburger Tor), I stared in awe at this magnificent eighteenth century neoclassical landmark. Above the gate sat a statue known as the "Quadriga," which depicted the goddess of victory driving a two-wheeled chariot pulled by four horses abreast.

Once through the gate, I took a cab to The Excelsior Hotel and checked into my hotel room at three p.m. This gave me three hours to settle in and prepare for the New Year's Eve Gala being held at the largest palace in Berlin, Charlottenburg Palace (Schloss Charlottenburg). My transportation for the evening was previously arranged.

Charlottenburg Palace, Grand Ballroom, Berlin, Germany

Germany's declining economy was not evident with the glitz and glamour of this beautiful venue. This palace was designed and constructed between 1695 and 1713. Enhancements were made during the eighteenth century. The inside was decorated in baroque and rococo styles.

I quickly perused the ballroom before making my entrance. President Paul von Hindenburg was eighty-two years old. He would not be present due to health issues. His son and confidant, Oskar von Hindenburg was to attend with his beautiful wife, Margarete von Marenholtz von Hindenburg.

Elite couples and singles, dressed to the nines, mingled while sipping cocktails and sampling hors d'oeuvres. Smoking was prevalent.

I managed to turn heads as I passed by. Men glanced up inquisitively and then resumed their conversations. Several pretty ladies smiled and I reciprocated. A server approached me; I accepted a glass of wine and several tempting appetizers.

As I worked the room, I nonchalantly eavesdropped on German and English conversations. Oskar was nearby; I patiently awaited the right moment to make my approach. My wait was brief; he spotted me and our eyes connected.

"Oskar von Hindenburg," he said as he extended his hand.

"Edmund Schmidt," I said. We shared a firm handshake.

"Of course, yes," Oskar said in English, "my father mentioned inviting you. We're extremely grateful to you for traveling so far. Did you have a pleasant journey?"

"Yes, thank you. I made all my connections and arrived early enough to rest before this party."

If he only knew my travel itinerary …

"Sprechen Sie deutsch?" Oskar asked me if I speak German.

In my best German dialect, I said that I speak German, English, French, Polish, Italian, and Spanish and asked his preference.

Oskar laughed exuberantly and reverted to English. "Incredible. I dabbled in languages; I'm fluent in German and English. My parents stressed a good education for my siblings and me. We can speak English, if you like. I'm curious, are you an interpreter?"

"I've worked as one, but I work mainly as an economist. My expertise is in helping people rebuild their fallen economies. It could be for a business, a city, or even an entire country. I take assignments throughout the United States and travel to other countries as well. I go whenever and wherever I'm needed."

"How fascinating. You have come to the right place. I must introduce you to my father. We're a military family in desperate need of economic expertise."

"I would be honored, Sir."

"Please call me Oskar. Did you arrive alone or bring a companion?"

"I'm single and I travelled here alone."

"Well, based on the glimpses I've noticed in your direction, I doubt if you'll be alone much during your stay." He nodded over his shoulder at several lovely young women giggling amongst themselves.

"You flatter me, Oskar. This is a splendid event. Beautiful ladies, handsome men, and such a grand palace. I'm here to help strengthen Germany's economy."

"Do you have a plan?"

"I have several, which I'll discuss in depth with you and your father."

"How rude of me, of course. We'll meet on this over the next several days. Tonight, we ring in 1930 at the stroke of midnight. Meanwhile, there's dinner and dancing and beautiful ladies."

"Never keep a lady waiting," I said. "I'm staying at The Excelsior Hotel, so reach out to me when you and your father are ready to meet."

"I will. Now mingle, join in the party. We'll talk soon."

As the evening proceeded and the champagne and other spirits flowed, the atmosphere grew very jovial. I danced and flirted with several ladies. At dinner, I was seated between two beautiful young women, Dorothea Schneider and Elise Keller. The three of us were fluent in German and English; we enjoyed lively conversations and dances.

I was careful not to divulge too much about myself to anyone, especially my economic mission. Only Oskar was privy to that topic tonight. The remaining guests only knew me as a visiting American. I had yet to win over President Hindenburg after all.

The party continued until well past three the next morning. I bid my farewells and headed back to my hotel for a good night's sleep. I was off to a great start and looked forward to my business meeting with the Hindenburgs.

I placed the "Do Not Disturb" door hanger outside my hotel room and slept in late. Following a wholesome brunch in one of my hotel's restaurants, I settled into a comfortable chair in the main lobby with a newspaper.

I speed read the news articles, searching for any pertinent information missing from my travel packet. A messenger appeared at my chair and said in English, "Edmund Schmidt, I have this envelope for you from Oskar von Hindenburg."

"Thank you," I said as I accepted the envelope and handed him a tip.

Oskar didn't waste any time. I was invited to meet with him and his father the following morning at nine. He scheduled a driver to pick me up at eight-thirty.

I was all set for the morning and decided to take a stroll around town. The weather was unseasonably warmer. Temperatures lingered around seven degrees Celsius. Looking in the storefront windows, I was shocked by all the vacant buildings and "going out of business" signs and banners. So many lives were impacted by these failed businesses.

I stepped into a coffee shop, purchased a coffee and streusel and took a seat at a small open table. My coffee and cake was excellent. It was relaxing sitting there reading the newspapers.

Then I saw her walk in. It was one of my dinner and dance companions from the previous evening, Elise Keller. She looked very chic in a forest green dress coat with matching hat and low-heeled black pumps.

Did she grow more beautiful overnight? Is she meeting someone? Should I approach her?

My questions were answered in no time. Our eyes met and she headed in my direction. Indeed, she had grown more beautiful overnight. I rose from my chair as she neared my table.

"Edmund, what a pleasant surprise," Elise said in English.

"Hello, Elise. How are you? Will you join me?"

"Yes, how nice."

I held her chair until she was comfortably seated. Our waiter appeared.

"I'd like a regular coffee and a slice of butter cake," she said.

"I just enjoyed a streusel; I've never tasted butter cake."

"Then you must," Elise said. "Two coffees and butter cakes, please."

We sat there for several hours—in our own little world of good coffee, cake, and conversation. It was getting close to dinner time.

"This is nice," I said. "I'd order more sweets, but I think we should have something more substantial. Are you free for dinner?"

"I'm sorry, no. My parents are expecting me. I'd love to some other time, though."

"We'll do that then," I said.

She left for her parents' home and I headed back to my hotel. After dinner, I laid out my clothes for the morning and called it a night.

*** * ***

Thursday morning, January 2, The Excelsior lobby

Oskar's driver picked me up promptly at eight-thirty in the morning and took me to the Reichstag Building (Reichstagsgebaude). The dedication DEM DEUTSCHEN VOLKE, meaning, "To the German people," can be seen on the frieze situated directly above the front entrance steps. Oskar greeted me as I stepped into the lobby.

"Good morning," he said. "I hope you're enjoying your stay so far."

"Oh, yes. What a beautiful morning."

"Yes, and a beautiful start to a new year."

Oskar led the way up several floors and down a few hallways. President Hindenburg's office suite was tastefully decorated in dark woods, leather and floor to ceiling tapestry draperies. Military and government paintings, maps and photographs adorned his spacious office walls. A tray filled with coffee and assorted biscuits was setup on a side table.

President Hindenburg rose from his chair as we entered the room.

"President Paul von Hindenburg, Edmund Schmidt," Oskar said.

"Welcome, Edmund. I'm pleased to meet you. Please call me, Paul," he said as he extended his hand.

"It's an honor to meet you, Paul." We shook hands.

First name basis at first meeting. I like this...

"First things first," Paul said. "Shall we have some refreshments before settling down to business?"

The three of us filled our cups and plates and gathered around Paul's desk.

"Edmund, thank you for joining us," Paul said. "Oskar and I share an aristocratic, military background. Since you have neither, I was skeptical initially when Chief of Staff Erich Ludendorff recommended you. After careful deliberation, however, I agreed that what Germany currently needs is a strong economist. You fit that requirement well. Tell me, are you prepared to stay on and help us?"

"Yes, I'll stay as long as you need me."

"Excellent, I've compiled this proprietary information for your review." He handed me an extremely thick, nondescript portfolio.

"Thank you," I said. "I'll guard this information at all times."

As I briefly leafed through the folder contents, I recognized the high points such as the agriculture, unemployment, and the infrastructure.

"I have a general sense of your situation," I said. "Once I've reviewed this file thoroughly, I'll make my recommendations."

"This portfolio provides the highlights," Paul said. "You'll have questions. Oskar is at your disposal day and night. He'll schedule our next meeting when you're ready."

Of course, the Hindenburgs have no idea that I already know the contents of this folder and more. I could reveal my plans for Germany right now but I won't. No, that would destroy this entire mission. I'll return to my hotel room and draw up a clear, high-level plan. Then we'll meet again and again and again until I gradually win them over ...

I worked into Sunday afternoon on my plan for Germany's economy. I had already been briefed for this mission and most of the high points were covered in my ongoing training courses. The little details, however, were news to me. The challenge would be to come across to the Hindenburgs as a person who previously knew very little about their plight. I carefully drafted my plan. Once written, I reviewed it in depth to ensure that I remained in the *present* time, (January 1930).

Monday morning, I phoned Oskar. He scheduled a noon meeting and arranged my transportation. Once I arrived, Oskar escorted me to his father's office.

"Oskar, Edmund, good afternoon," Paul said. "I took the liberty of ordering lunch in for us."

"How thoughtful of you," I said.

The three of us fixed our plates and coffees and got down to business.

"Edmund, I'm impressed that you survived a portfolio of this magnitude so quickly," Paul said.

"Experience and I've always been a fast reader," I said. "Would you like to hear my findings to date?"

"Definitely," Paul said.

"I reviewed all the information in your file. First, a little back history leading up to our current dilemma. The United States and European economies are failing miserably. Everyone is trying to recover from the war. Due to lost revenues and neglected agriculture, adults and children are dying from starvation and illnesses.

"The Wall Street stock market crash further crippled the world. People are standing in bread-lines and begging for food and money. Even upstanding citizens are resorting to crime out of desperation.

"Unemployment rates have reached record highs throughout Europe and the United States. The homeless rates are steadily increasing. Businesses are closing. The usual imports and exports between countries have ceased. Loans are not available. A universal moral and morale decline is apparent.

"The Great Depression is upon all of us and the world is indeed in a dismal state. As depressing and negative as all of this sounds, I have a solution. Do either of you have any questions before I proceed?"

"No," Oskar and Paul said in unison.

I paused for some water and resumed. "I'd like to begin with agriculture. You have excellent farms that could easily feed all your people in addition to exporting foods.

"Your farmers need financial help to get back on their feet. Money is tight now, but if you were to adjust some government expenses to help your farmers, Germany would benefit. As your agriculture improves, exporting will eventually resume."

"Excellent point," Paul said. "We must rebuild our peoples' health and grow strong from within."

"Definitely. My next topic is unemployment," I said. "Only your wealthy can afford luxuries. Everyone needs non-luxury items, such as food, medicine, medical care, education, and job training. I believe that given sufficient work opportunities, average male and female workers would choose legitimate jobs over illegal activities. Could your budget be reworked to help your grocers, butchers, pharmacies, medical offices, hospitals, and schools?"

"I believe with your help, we could move in that direction," Paul said. "At the very least, we could offer tax incentives to business owners."

"Yes, exactly," I said. "If your business owners paid lower taxes, they could hire more people. The unemployment rate would go down. Increased employment would result in less federal subsidizing, home foreclosures, and bankruptcies."

"Interesting ...," Oskar said.

"Creative accounting is my specialty," I said. "Now, if we can boost the agriculture and get the basic businesses going, you'll have a nation of healthy, strong people who have access to essential products. The providers of these products will need workers which will gradually lower the unemployment rate."

"Yes," Paul said, "it could take a miracle to fund all these ideas, but I like what I'm hearing. Our morals and morale will improve with legitimate jobs for all our able-bodied adults, regardless of gender or religious beliefs."

"Jewish business owners look up to you, Paul," I said, "as their protector from Hitler and the infiltration of Nazi anti-semantic propaganda."

"I had a strict upbringing," Paul said. "Raised a Lutheran from a long line of aristocratic militants. Eighty-two years old, I'm more conservative than today's youth regarding homosexuals, transvestites, liberal entertainment, and such. I do *not*, however, blame the Jews for the downfall of our country. Nor do I align with Hitler or the Nazis."

"Have you suffered any consequences as a result?"

"No, not yet. Hitler's greed and narcissism far outweigh his intelligence. He's a mere painter from Austria and a social misfit. Still, he has followers. He's been patiently lying in wait for the right moment to make his next move. Mark my words, he has his eye on Germany and the rest of the world. I wouldn't trust Hitler as far as I could throw him."

"I agree. The world nervously watches Hitler. He must be kept at bay," I said. "Shall we proceed?" I asked both men.

"Yes," Paul and Oskar said in unison.

"Next on my list is infrastructure. Are you interested in repairing and rebuilding your roads and bridges and improving your public transportation system?"

"We definitely need this," Paul said, "especially since the war. I expect we could reduce our military budget, at least temporarily. The last thing Germany needs right now is another war."

"I don't know the figures yet," I said, "but if you agree, we'll rework the budget and taxes. Perhaps some of your military funds could be redirected to these improvements since you're in peace time. Only if necessary, we'll research loans.

"Here are some of the benefits that I foresee with an improved infrastructure. New jobs will be created. Transportation to, from, and throughout Germany will be increased and safer. The increased transportation will result in new businesses, housing and schools sprouting up. The tourist trade will also benefit.

"These are my main points so far. Basically, I believe that Germany, or any country for that matter, is nothing without its people. A thriving country needs healthy, strong people.

"To remain strong, people need food, shelter, clothing, education, medical care, and good morale; they need jobs to pay for these things. So, if we build up your people from within and give businesses a jump start, your people will return to work and the economy will turn around.

"Your thoughts, gentlemen?"

Paul appeared deep in thought for several minutes. He sat quietly and fiddled with his handlebar mustache. "Prior to your arrival, Oskar, my immediate staff and I discussed our situation to death. We're all so engulfed in the thick of things, that we couldn't come up with a plausible solution. Whereas, you, a total stranger, succeeded. Your plan is sound and feasible. My only regret is not engaging your services sooner."

"I appreciate your approval, Paul," I said. "We can't change the past, but we can alter the future. Remember, I drafted this plan based on known facts and my professional projections. As a preliminary plan, it's not cast in stone. If we run into obstacles, we'll discuss other options. I'm ready to get started whenever you are."

Paul and Oskar rose from their chairs and I followed suit. We shook hands and toasted the deal with brandy.

*** * ***

I arrived back at my hotel earlier than expected and decided to phone Elise.

She picked up on the second ring. "Hello," Elise said cheerfully.

"Greetings, Elise," I said. "How are you?"

"Oh, Edmund, good, and you?"

"Very well, thank you. I know this is short notice ... would you like to join me for dinner tonight ... and perhaps see a film?"

"Why, yes, that sounds like fun," she said. "I can meet you in your hotel lobby in about an hour."

"See you then."

It was a beautiful evening for a stroll around town. Elise and I walked along, engaged in pleasant conversation, pausing now and then to take in our surroundings. We briskly passed a group of desperate looking ladies of the evening.

Once out of earshot, Elise said, "Men and children also do this for survival."

"Children should be in school, supported by their parents or guardians. Able-bodied adults should have legitimate jobs and training programs."

"It sounds like you have great ideas for our people."

"Indeed, I do."

I could be falling for this woman. What lies ahead?

She picked an excellent family-run restaurant and ordered for both of us. This may have been the most substantial meal of my life. I was grateful for the after-dinner walk to the cinema. *Asphalt*, one of Germany's final silent films was playing. I was so taken by this film that I didn't mind the subtitles. We enjoyed the film immensely.

Walking back, holding hands, Elise asked, "Tell me, Edmund, how do our films measure up to the ones you see back home?"

"Very well," I said. "I truly enjoy the cinema and would go more often if I could."

"Yes, I know, our lives are so busy with work and other nonsense."

I had fun tonight. Spontaneous, interesting, and hassle free. Elise is wonderful. Must be careful, though. I'm only here short term and the last thing we need is to break each other's hearts. We'd best remain casual friends.

*** * ***

Over the course of the next several weeks, Oskar escorted me around to meet all the farmers and document their concerns. They needed financial support and full or part-time workers. The latter wouldn't be a problem with the current unemployment rate.

We visited local businesses and discussed survival options. They all needed financial help and workers. Yet another employment plus.

The infrastructure seriously needed restoration. Soon, public transportation would be available throughout Germany. This would boost employment, businesses, housing, the tourist trade, and the overall economy.

The morale was at a record low. Unemployed adults were fed up with sitting idle and watching their dreams evaporate. They were open to learning new skills and trades. Change was good.

Filling the new jobs wouldn't be an issue. Funding all these projects would be the real challenge. Paul, Oskar, and I met regularly to discuss the budget and ways to re-structure it. The new peacetime military budget freed up monies for agriculture, businesses and infrastructure. Personal and business taxes were reduced nationwide.

The Hindenburgs also agreed to tighten government spending on non-essential projects and establish priorities. The country needed to get back on its feet. People required the basics of food, clothing, shelter, and health care. The *nice-to-have* projects would be considered later.

We were actively researching loan and export possibilities. The United States and other countries recovering from World War I expenditures banned loans and imports. Business exchange would eventually return between countries. In the interim, each country had to take care of its own.

*** * ***

One day, while investigating areas in need of improvement, Oskar took me aside. "I have something to confide in you," he said, "but you are sworn to secrecy, especially from my father."

"What is it, Oskar? ... Are you ill?"

"No, nothing like that. It's regarding Hitler and the Nazi party. You're familiar with my father's feelings toward Hitler and the Nazis. I agree with my father on most counts. The Nazi party, however, stirs up some questions within me. I attended several of their meetings to learn more about them."

"Learning is a good thing, but I highly recommend that you remain cautious of this organization. Are you interested in joining them?"

"No, I don't believe so. I do not align with the Nazi party. Their popularity, however, makes me curious. You must not tell my father."

"Your secret is safe with me. Do be careful, though. Your father's age and health issues could interfere with his governing abilities. You need each other right now. I do not trust Hitler, the Nazi party or their empty promises. Germany needs strong leadership from within—not to be governed by Hitler and the Nazi party."

"I agree," Oskar said, "and with your help, Germany will regain strength and prosper once again."

*** * ***

Moving forward, Oskar never brought up Hitler or the Nazi party in our conversations. He and I worked long days, nights and weekends together. Fallen farms were beginning to recover. Crews were hired and ready to begin refurbishing the infrastructure. Paul, Oskar and staff worked diligently to revamp the government's budget. Sufficient funds were allocated to set our plans in motion. The overall morale of Germany was beginning to rise.

Reichstag building, President Paul Hindenburg's office

"Our agricultural, business, and infrastructure programs are underway," I said to the Hindenburgs. "Morale is up and I have some ideas on maintaining this."

"Please continue," Paul said.

"We're social beings by nature. People need interaction with families and friends. Why not create social organizations that provide services and activities for adults and children?"

"What types of organizations?" Paul asked.

"Children's sports teams that play for fun and competitively."

"Hmmh ..." Paul said, "I was a cadet at age twelve. Yes, children need discipline and stamina."

"In addition to team spirit and health benefits," Oskar said, "but, how would we fund these organizations?"

"I would suggest starting small," I said. "Our local businesses and private benefactors could sponsor the youths' teams. Parents and teachers could volunteer their time as coaches."

Paul and Oskar nodded affirmatively, and Oskar said, "We're behind this idea. Do you have any other suggestions?"

"Yes, with parents returning to work and many single parent families, I think after school programs would be useful. Schools, libraries, even churches might have some rooms where children could do school work, or receive tutoring until their parents finish work. Volunteers could supervise the children. Schools could possibly budget hiring some assistants or tutors."

"Another good idea," Paul said.

"Besides keeping the children on track scholastically, it keeps them safe and occupied," Oskar said.

"Then there's the teenagers and adults," I said. "Teenagers and senior citizens have special needs as do younger adults. Support groups benefit people suffering from many things such as depression, divorce, and addictions."

"How will we find qualified helpers for these types of programs?" Oskar asked.

"Churches, for starters," I said. "Ministers of all faiths are trained counselors. Social workers—your colleges and college students should consider this high demand field."

"I envision this working," Oskar said. "Ministers could conduct group and private sessions inside their churches. We wouldn't need to wait for new buildings to initiate the programs. The war and economy has taken a toll on our people. Yes, we need these types of programs."

"We're Lutheran," Paul said, "but we tolerate all religions. Our programs should include people of all faiths."

"Of course," I said.

"We especially disagree with Hitler and Nazi party anti-semantic teachings," Oskar said.

"I do not trust Hitler," Paul said.

"Nor do I," Oskar said.

"Gentlemen, our consensus on Hitler and the Nazis," I said, "is that we will rebuild Germany from within and not be deceived by their lies."

Farewell meeting with Paul and Oskar Hindenburg

"Edmund," Paul said, "Please come in and make yourself comfortable. Oskar and I were just discussing our progress. We couldn't have done this without you."

"Thank you both," I said. "I'm honored to have met you and very pleased with our progress. We made a great team."

"Indeed," Oskar said. "Would you like to stay on a bit longer or must you rush back now? You're welcome to stay as long as you like."

"Thank you, gentlemen. I have grown quite fond of you and your fair city, but I must consider my home and work responsibilities."

"Do you know your next assignment?" Paul asked.

"No, not yet," I said. "I should know within the next couple of days."

"Would you stop home before heading to your new assignment?" Oskar asked.

"It all depends on the location and when the client needs me."

"Such an exciting life you lead," Oskar said, "traveling around the globe, helping so many people."

My cheeks felt warm; I was flattered by Oskar's remark. "My lifestyle's not for everyone, but it works for me. There's rarely a dull moment."

With that, Oskar poured three brandies.

"Prost!" We toasted heartily.

I excused myself and headed back to my hotel.

*** * ***

After Edmund left, Oskar stayed on to speak privately with his father.

"I've grown attached to Edmund," Paul said, "as though he was my second son or nephew. He proved himself quite amicably, especially as a commoner."

"With all due respect, Father, there is *nothing* common about Edmund. Despite not having an aristocratic or military background, his socio-economic expertise far surpasses anyone I've ever known. We need men of his caliber. Our friend Edmund has a heavy decision to make."

"A difficult one at that. He's accustomed to living in America. It's quite different there."

"Yes, but he's multilingual and seems quite comfortable here. I happen to know that he'll also miss a special lady should he leaves us."

"He's met someone? I'm not surprised. Do I know her?" Paul asked.

"Elise Keller. They met his first night here at our New Year's Eve party. I've seen them together around town on numerous occasions."

"Have you approached either of them?"

"No, never. They were always heavily engrossed in conversation and laughter and appeared to be very much in love."

"Interesting," Paul said. "Perhaps, he will decide to extend his stay."

After Oskar left, Paul phoned Chief of Staff Erich Ludendorff. "Thank you for recommending Edmund Schmidt," Paul said. "He did a thorough job of planning our recovery. We're in the process of implementing his plans. I feel very positive about the outcome. Oskar and I have asked him to stay on. He needs to think it over."

"Of course. Would you like me to speak to him?" Ludendorff asked.

"I don't want him to feel pressured into staying. Does your American contact also control Edmund's work schedule?" Paul asked.

"Hmmh… Let me see what I can do."

*** * ***

The Excelsior Hotel, Berlin, Germany

I found myself pacing my hotel room and decided to take a walk around town to get some fresh air and ponder my situation. My job here is done. I am free to leave. It shouldn't be long before I'm off on some new adventure. Paul is still doing well. He's worked his whole life. It's time for him to hand over the reins to Oskar or Ludendorff.

Then there's Elise. Would we miss each other dearly, or was this just an infatuation between two lonely adults who met by chance in an oppressive post-war setting? If I return home, could Elise and I cross paths again in the future or in the past? If so, would we remember our time here together or be total strangers? Would we be available and open to a new relationship?

I've never stayed anywhere beyond completing a mission. What would I be giving up by staying here? Well, there's my home with the hefty mortgage balance and ever-increasing taxes. I have some family and friends, but they're currently scattered all over the world.

Then there's all the advances between 1930 and 2015. Could I give up the significant medical advancements? What if Elise, God forbid, becomes terminally ill and there's no cure in sight? Could I live knowing that the cure for her illness was successfully implemented during my lifetime?

Technologies have also grown tremendously since 1930. I am accustomed, or I should say addicted, to all my techie gadgets and conveniences. They weren't always present. Somehow, I survived prior to their time.

Yes, it was frustrating at times during my stay here. I'd go to reach for one of my devices out of habit. To my credit, I managed remarkably well without them.

Manufacturing has changed a lot also. Cars, clothing, furniture, all types of things. Food manufacturing has gotten out of hand with all our processed and genetically modified organism, (GMO) foods.

Consumer awareness is at an all-time high regarding the importance of complete food product ingredient labels and free-range farming without antibiotics, hormones, and pesticides. I'd trade all the food safety issues back home for all natural, free-range farming here in a heartbeat.

My 2014 car has more bells and whistles than cars from the 1930s. The cars that I've seen on this mission, however, are built for the climate and roads here.

I'm beginning to think that my stress level would drop drastically by reversing time—even to a post-war, depressed economy.

One thing for certain, if I return to my former life, I must do so alone. I cannot take Elise or anyone else with me. What should I do?

*** * ***

It didn't take long to make up my mind. I was about to contact my employer when they contacted me. My next assignment was to stay on and oversee the implementation of my plans for Germany. The choice was mine. Should I refuse this mission, I'll return home tomorrow morning and await some alternate assignment.

*** * ***

Six months later…

Greetings, Edmund Schmidt speaking. My plans for Germany are being implemented in full force. The farms are no longer in ruins. Workers are back on the job. The infrastructure is being rebuilt. The economy is showing steady growth. Businesses are rebuilding and new ones are springing up. Social organizations are gaining popularity. German morale is on the rise. I'm proud to say, mission accomplished …

I drove to Elise's apartment this Friday afternoon and we headed on our way. It was a splendid day for a road trip with my wonderful companion. Elise and I talked and joked and enjoyed the breathtaking scenery.

This well-deserved getaway has been in the works for some time now. Finally, the day has arrived. We're on our way to a relaxing weekend in the countryside, just the two of us; the timing could not be better ...

"It is not in the stars to hold our destiny but in ourselves."

— William Shakespeare

Epilogue

The signing of the Versailles Treaty marked the end of World War I and all wars. German government accepted citizens of all races, creeds and ethnic backgrounds.

Hitler and the Nazi party eventually fizzled out. The world was spared the Holocaust and evacuation of the Jews. The Brandenburg Gate symbolized European unity and peace before its time. Imagine how this turn of events would have altered the history of the world.

If you can imagine the above, challenge your mind even deeper. Think of our world without poverty, dictatorships, monarchies, communism, weapons, wars, and disputes. Economies flourish. People are healthy, educated, and happy. Imagine, if you can, a world at peace ...

Always

My name is Marla and I have an interesting story to tell. An avid traveler, I've always enjoyed visiting new places, meeting new people and learning all about them. Are they healthy? What do they eat and drink? What language(s) do they speak? How do they dress? Do they pursue careers and obtain their training in colleges, trade schools, or both?

I prep for my trips as much as possible. Multilingual, I'm comfortable with the local language or take a crash travel course. The romance languages generally roll off my tongue. Assuming I understand at least a third of a native's dialogue, we communicate well.

Planes, trains, and automobiles have taken me throughout the United States—North, South, East, Central and West. A handful of states remain on my bucket list. I've also traveled by land and sea throughout Europe, South America, Canada and the Caribbean. Most of my trips were positive. Occasionally travel delays or bad weather created glitches. Mere inconveniences, nothing more.

I'm departing today on an exciting adventure with people I've missed for a very long time. While maneuvering traffic en route to my local train station, I mentally reviewed my upcoming connections. I had to make the next train. Otherwise, my narrow window of opportunity would close. I won't let this happen. No, never.

I reached the train outbound track in record time. Ticket secured in my jacket zippered pocket, I boarded the train and quickly claimed a seat. The train rolled in to station after station, passengers alighted, passengers boarded. I remained; I still had a ways to go …

How will this secret place look? Will it be serenely beautiful as displayed in the movies? Will *they* be there? For how long? When my time is up, will I be anxious to leave or wish I could stay? Can I stay?

The intercom just announced, "Next station stop, Harrison." That's the last announced stop. Mine must be next or coming up soon. I patiently watched as the remaining passengers alighted. The train sat still for several minutes and then all the doors closed. I was the only passenger on this train. My heart raced and I experienced dry mouth and rubber legs. In a few minutes, I'll know …

As I stepped off the train, a thick fog enveloped me. All traces of the train, track, and platform disappeared. The ground felt cushy beneath my feet. No sounds, smells, buildings, people, or animals. Is this it, or did I leave the train too soon?

Navigating the fog was challenging. I lost all sense of direction. Ten minutes, maybe longer, went by before the fog thinned enough to reveal my surroundings. It was like exiting a dark tunnel and stepping out into bright sunlight. I spotted a glistening white archway in the distance and headed toward it.

Upon reaching the archway, I paused. This must be it. Surely, I found my meeting location. It was so quiet and peaceful standing there. The temperature was comfortable with low humidity. My allergies were absent.

I paced back and forth, keeping my eyes out for someone, something, any type of sign that my time has come. And then it happened. Classical music played softly in the background. I anxiously awaited what was coming next. This was my first visit to Heaven. I felt privileged, thrilled and frightened all in one …

*** * ***

My mom was the first person to greet me. She looked radiantly happy and healthy. Her flowing white gown and long dark hair had tiny pink rosebud embellishments. Delicate curls framed her beautiful young face. We embraced and then walked to a park like setting. Endless lush green for as far as the eyes could see. We sat side by side on a bench situated beneath a treed archway.

"Marla, oh, Marla, I miss you so," my mom said. "You look wonderful, dear. I'm so happy you're doing so well."

"I miss you too, Mom. You are so beautiful." Tears trickled down my face as we embraced ever so tightly.

"I'm so happy for Tara and Michael."

"How did you know?"

"They were very much in love before I passed. I'm not one to miss my granddaughter's wedding."

"No, you're not. We knew you were right there with us. Tara and I sensed it. Others did too."

"I know. Father O'Sullivan, and many others. They dared not voice their feelings for fear of upsetting Tara's special day. I've been watching you, your sisters, brothers, their spouses, and kids. You're all so active and doing well."

"That's for sure. There's never a dull moment. The kids are growing up way too fast. The years just fly by."

"Yes, they do, especially in eternity."

"Eternity, infinity, always–no beginning or end. It's all so mysterious. I can only imagine …"

"One day you'll understand. You're all strong and dedicated. I'm so proud of all of you. Sometimes I worry still…but that's what mothers do."

"Please don't worry about us, Mom … I wish I could stay here."

"When your time comes, you will. Until then, your loved ones need you and you need them. You still have many things to do."

"I do keep busy."

"Yes, you do. I don't know how you stay on top of everything, but you do it well. I'm so proud of you."

"Ah, Mom, I learned from the best, you and Dad."

"Your dad and I love all of you so much. We'll be with you always."

"Did you ever visit us as a cardinal couple?" I asked.

"Yes, many times both individually and together. I hope you enjoy our singing. We've been practicing some new duets, so stay *tuned.*"

"You're too funny and yes, you both sing beautifully."

"All of you have decks and we do stand out nicely against the snow."

"I'll say. Speaking of snow. You know, of course, about our crazy, unpredictable weather. Every time we have a chain of snow falls, we always think of you two. You always enjoyed looking out the windows at the newly fallen snow."

"We can't take credit for *all* of your snow falls, but between your father and I and our old cold country cronies, we certainly orchestrated some good ones." She flashed me her most contagious smile.

"You know, after you and Dad passed, I had several intense dreams of both of you. You were both young and healthy. I'd say in your mid-twenties. You were probably engaged or maybe newlyweds."

"Do you remember anything about these dreams?"

"They seemed brief. I'm not sure as I was sleeping. Black and white images of both of you smiling and hugging each other. I remember the two of you dancing. It wasn't your wedding. You and Dad were dressed nicely but not in formal wear. These dreams all ended so intensely that I was startled awake."

"You were frightened? We never meant to scare you. How did they end?"

"Regardless of the snip-its I recall from each dream, they always ended with you and Dad going up an escalator that appeared to be surrounded by puffy white clouds. You stood arm in arm on this rising stairway and turned smiling and waving goodbye. Then you were gone ..."

"I remember paying you some visits back then. Your dad and I couldn't say goodbye to any of you. I knew that you had prior encounters with a few spirits who passed before us. We just wanted to let you know that we're in a better place. I knew that you would pass the word on to the others."

"Yes," I said in a trembling voice, "I did tell our immediate family and they were relieved. They've also had signs here and there from you two ... I just love your gown, hair, and shoes. You look like a princess."

"I feel like Cinderella at the ball. I always wished I could sweep my hair up like this and don a long flowing gown and strappy heels and dance the night away with my handsome prince."

"And now you do. I'm so happy for you and Dad. This is all so new to me. I could be pulled back at any given moment. In case I don't see Dad this time, please give him my love."

"Yes, dear. In case you're wondering, he already knows. Don't be a stranger. Come back as often as you can and send the others up. You're always welcome here."

Her arms surrounded me and the essence of honeysuckle filled my every pore. It was one of her favorite fragrances; she wore it often. We embraced once more and I felt her presence gradually slipping away. I think she was somewhere nearby. But I could no longer see or feel her. The honeysuckle scent was less intense but still present ...

I sat quietly on the bench for several minutes. Or had it been hours? Time seemed to stand still here. It was eternity after all. The lush green archway of trees over my bench fanned me with gentle breezes. Classical music played in surround sound.

*** * ***

My dad smiled broadly as he tipped his cap and sat down beside me. He was smartly dressed in a medium blue denim shirt and jeans.

"Dad, oh, I miss you so much." We hugged and kissed.

"My baby girl, you're doing well. Please don't cry."

"Sorry," I sobbed. "Tears of joy. I just saw Mom and now you. I can't believe this." My face was saturated from crying.

He held me close. "It's so good to see you again in person. Your mom and I keep tabs on all of you. I don't think we miss much."

"I'm sure you don't. Maybe when you're praying or resting. Other than that, I guess we keep you pretty busy."

"I'll say. We're always aware of our earthling loved ones and much too busy to rest."

"No sleep or illness or medicine or food—so different here."

"Yes, and peaceful. I remember you kids asking me what I wanted for Christmas or Father's Day. I would answer, 'Peace and quiet.' " He was laughing heartily at this point. "You poor kids were bewildered. 'Where can we get *peace and quiet?*' you cried out."

"Yes, hearing you say this takes me back there. Seems like yesterday. You're so young and handsome, Dad. I love your cap." My tears evolved into a broad smile. "You know, I often picture you in one of your baseball caps. You had so many great ones and wore them all the time."

My dad laughed contagiously. "Well, I started wearing caps for sun protection. Guess they grew on me. No skin damage worries here. I just keep wearing them."

"They're *you.* I just saw Mom. She looks so beautiful and healthy. Do you ever see each other?"

"Always."

"How about your parents, siblings, and other relatives?"

"Yes, and my old friends and your mom's relatives and friends, our school teachers and old neighbors ... Your mom and I know so many people here. We're never lonely."

"I'm so happy for you two. You're both so healthy and serene. Tell me if I'm wrong, but I've seen some signs from both of you."

"Tell me about them," my dad said, grinning.

"Well, a number of us sensed both of you at Tara's wedding."

"Sure, we wouldn't miss it."

"There's also been butterflies. One day when I was driving home from work in my last car, on an extremely hot and humid day, I couldn't use the air conditioner. The car was idling rough and threatening to die any minute.

"Out of nowhere, a beautiful yellow, orange, and brown butterfly landed on my driver's side mirror. As I crawled along in bumper-to-bumper traffic, I couldn't stop glancing over at this beautiful creature. Even when traffic picked up, my new companion stayed with me until I pulled into my garage and turned off the ignition key. My guardian from above ..."

"I was worried about you driving around in that old car. It served you well, but it was time to trade it in. You made a good choice, by the way. What possessed you to keep all your cars so long?"

"I don't know, maybe you and Mom. You two were always frugal. Besides, cars grow on you, like comfortable old shoes. You sure did like working on your cars. We have some great old black and white photos of you with some of them."

"Yes, I did," my dad said with a chuckle.

"Oh, my electrical at home. Every so often, on a perfectly clear day, I've experienced a sudden power outage or new light bulbs shorting out. Just me–not my neighbors. Sound familiar?"

"I'm just saying, 'Hi' or reminding you to turn off the lights you're not using."

"I knew it."

"Your mom and I really miss all of you and we're so proud. Sometimes we worry still…"

"Worry? No, Dad, please don't worry about any of us. You and Mom did that long enough."

"Your lives are so stressful and those technical gadgets… They make your lives easier but so complicated."

"What do you mean?"

"Well, your gizmos help you do things faster, but they also eliminate jobs. And instead of spending quality time together, people just send messages, or chat on their gizmos."

"That's for sure. My friends rarely meet for lunch or even talk on the phone anymore. Then, when we finally get together, within a few minutes, everyone's checking their phones. Why even get together?"

"It's starting younger and younger—even our pre-school great-grandkids."

"I hear music again," I said. "Is that a harp? How beautiful."

"Yes, music is always playing here. We love you, sweetie, always ..." He wrapped his arms around me and hugged me ever so tightly, a little looser, loosely, ... and then he was gone. Gone, just like my mom ...

*** * ***

When I booked this journey, I knew that it would be brief. Transfers to and from were limited. When my time was up, it was up. My visits with my parents were magical. Still, there's my grandparents, aunts, uncles, friends–so many people I know here. I hope to come back again. Yes, I will return ...

Alone now, sitting on the bench, I closed my eyes and concentrated on the soothing music and calming breezes. Ten minutes, twenty minutes went by. I'm not sure as there's no sense of time in eternity. The next thing I knew, I was standing on a train platform waiting for my train home. Not a soul in sight.

The train pulled in shortly. As I boarded the train, the conductor greeted me with a smile. I guess he knew all about this secret train stop or maybe he just sensed something special about this place. I walked to an empty car and sat quietly until I heard my station announced.

Driving home from the train station, the sun was blazing. I grabbed my sunglasses and placed them on my face. Then out of nowhere, *BOOM*– thunder, lightning, and a heavy downpour of rain. I couldn't see a thing despite my high-speed windshield wipers. Then it happened–a double rainbow arched the sky straight ahead. Well, if that wasn't a sign from above …

My mind was spinning all the way home. I couldn't stop smiling about my day. Home at last, safe, sound, and dazed—I was torn between taking a nap and running a marathon.

Today was the most extraordinary day of my entire life. Prior to experiencing Heaven firsthand, my mind perceived it to be as depicted in movies and stories written by survivors who experienced a glimpse of life on the other side.

I must say their descriptions of beauty and serenity were close. I had envisioned the radiance, soothing music, calming breezes, lush greenery and a special bench reserved for visitors and their resident loved ones. Heaven exceeded everything that I could possibly imagine. Does Heaven look the same to all visitors or does it vary based on their expectations?

Is there really an afterlife or is life as we know it on Earth all there is? Should all the stories and movies about life after death and reincarnation be categorized as science fiction? Is there an ounce of truth in any of them? Who amongst us hasn't posed these questions?

Whether you believe that the universe and all life within it stems from a higher being or align with the theory of evolution, we are here for a reason. Do we only live one life, die and evaporate into the universe or are we reincarnated after death? Does Heaven exist? How about Hell or Purgatory?

*** * ***

It's been several months since I visited my parents. Time flies in good times and bad. Sometimes when I have a quiet moment, I reflect on that special visit and smile. Will there ever come a time when we experience Heaven on Earth? It's highly unlikely. Besides, this would eliminate Heaven and we wouldn't want to do that.

Winter settled in with lower than average temperatures and frequent snow storms. My parents and their cold weather cohorts must be delirious. I donned my toasty-warm robe and slippers and headed to the kitchen. Today was my parents' wedding anniversary–their seventy-fifth to be exact. Would they send us a sign today?

I opened the window blinds overlooking my rear deck and smiled warmly. The snow ceased falling, at least for now. There had to be a foot or more on the ground—a pure white blanket of shimmering diamonds in the sun.

Mr. and Mrs. Cardinal perched on the railing singing an especially beautiful duet. I pressed my face against the window pane and listened intently to the love birds tune. Suddenly, I froze in my tracks. Could this be? My eyes welled up with tears as I listened to them sing "Always"–their wedding song ...

www.ingramcontent.com/pod-product-compliance
Lightning Source LLC
Chambersburg PA
CBHW022117170626
46808CB00002B/757